JUST US

A Lodge Series Novel

J.H. CROIX

This is a work of fiction. Names, characters, businesses, places, events and incidents are either the products of the author's imagination or used in a fictitious manner. Any resemblance to actual persons, living or dead, or actual events is purely coincidental.

Cover design by Najla Qamber Designs

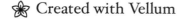 Created with Vellum

This one goes out to every good story that happened after something went wrong. Sometimes those are the best moments. Don't miss out.

Sign up for my newsletter for information on new releases & get a FREE copy of one of my books!

http://jhcroixauthor.com/subscribe/

Follow me!
jhcroix@jhcroix.com
https://amazon.com/author/jhcroix
https://www.bookbub.com/authors/j-h-croix
https://www.facebook.com/jhcroix
https://www.instagram.com/jhcroix/

was arguing with me because he didn't want to pay for a new room. I couldn't believe this.

He pressed on. "It's on my credit card. If I have to, I'll ask the staff to escort you out of that room. Cheryl and I are staying there."

Although anger was buoying me through this dreadful encounter, a sense of defeat washed over me. The room *had* been reserved on his credit card, and I'd conveniently blanked out that detail. I should've known he would use the trip because he was selfish, incredibly selfish.

My cheeks were hot, and I was tired. I glanced wildly around, looking for a rescue I knew wouldn't come. Las Vegas was so crowded, no one appeared to be batting an eye at this argument taking place in front of them. People just stepped around us and kept on walking. I closed my eyes, taking a deep breath and intending to say something sensible, although there really was nothing sensible to say.

At that moment, I felt a hand slide down my back. I opened my eyes, reflexively glancing up. My breath caught in my throat as I stared into the eyes of the most handsome man I'd ever seen. He had deep green eyes and amber hair glinting under the lights from above. He wore a suit, and, oh man, did he ever wear it well.

The black jacket stretched across his broad shoulders. There was a flicker of recognition for me, but I couldn't place how I knew this man.

"There you are, Ellie," he said smoothly. "I was just looking for you."

Staring at him, I couldn't say why, but I knew this man had overheard my interaction with Wayne and was stepping in to somehow save me from further embarrassment.

"Oh," I finally managed. "Well, you found me."

Looking into this man's eyes sent my belly into a series of flips and electric heat spinning through my veins. I wasn't sure what to say next because I didn't know what the story was.

This man—tall, sexy, and exuding confidence—turned, his eyes narrowing as he looked Wayne up and down.

"Jacob Taylor," he said with a nod, appearing to be introducing himself to Wayne. He didn't extend a hand and gave off a frosty, cool energy.

My brain pinged. Jacob Taylor was a tech billionaire. He owned a company dedicated to online security. Rumor had it he started the company after his sister died in a tragic accident that was caused by a man she met over some dating app. He was quite media shy, although his face had been in the news more than enough. Aside from seeing photographs of him, my recognition came from briefly seeing him at a distance, once, during a function in Seattle.

I used to live in Bellingham, Washington, but I'd moved to Seattle a few years ago. My brother, the only family I had left, lived in Seattle and ran a security company. He had collaborated with Jacob on a few projects. I hadn't met Jacob that night because I had only been there briefly, begging off and telling my brother, Aidan, that it was a bit much for me.

Wayne stared at Jacob for a moment and appeared to make the same connection I did. He managed a tight smile. "Nice to meet you. Wayne Bradley," he said, holding out his hand.

If Jacob hadn't made his point before, it became abundantly clear now. His eyes flicked down to Wayne's outstretched hand and back to his face. "No offense, but I don't intend to shake your hand. It appears you're being an asshole to someone who matters a lot to me. But no worry. You can have your shitty room. Ellie forgot I had reserved the penthouse suite tonight."

Wayne looked from me to Jacob, his eyes widening.

I replied, "I didn't forget. I just wasn't intending to let him use that room."

At this point, my ex-friend, Cheryl, approached. "What's going on?" she asked, her gaze curious as she looked from Wayne to Jacob to me.

My pride was stinging. Not because I wanted Wayne back, but it still stung to have someone I once called my friend screw around with my boyfriend behind my back.

Jacob's arm slid around my waist, pulling me against his side. He was warm and strong, and my entire body was tingling from his nearness. I didn't know what to make of any of this, but I was going with it.

Wayne opened his mouth to reply, but Jacob's voice—clear, authoritative, and dismissive—cut across. "What's going on is your asshole of a boyfriend, who fucked around with you, is arguing over the room. It's all yours, sweetheart."

Although I was a little freaked out that Jacob appeared to know that much information about me, it was a rather glorious moment. Cheryl's cheeks flushed, and her eyes took on a mutinous glint. I didn't know what led Jacob to intervene here, but in this slice of time, I was getting a small bit of payback.

"Let's go," he said, incrementally tightening his arm around my waist. I felt the heat of his touch through my thin silk blouse.

Seeing as there was no particularly graceful way to exit the situation, I simply followed his lead. Unlike when I was trying to make my way through the crowded spaces by myself, Jacob's mere presence seemed to cause the crowd to part before us.

He didn't say a word, but his touch was firm, and in a matter of minutes, we were standing in front of a bank of elevators. He tapped the button and, as if by magic, the elevator doors whispered open. Another miracle, no one was inside. Still tingling all over, and a bit stunned, I stepped ahead of him to the elevator when he exerted a gentle pressure on my lower back.

Once we were alone in the elevator, I had no idea what to say. I looked up to find his rich green gaze waiting. I thought perhaps I was crazy, but my body sure thought there was desire in his eyes.

Now you know you're crazy. There is no way on God's green earth that Jacob Taylor wants you.

I had a hard time getting air. Not to mention, my pulse was going wild.

"Thank you," I finally managed.

Jacob smiled, just barely, glancing away from me and asking, "What floor?"

I was befuddled for a beat before asking, "For my room?"

It suddenly occurred to me I had just let a man who was almost a complete stranger take me into an elevator. He was now asking me where my room was. The only reason I didn't totally freak out was because I knew Aidan considered him a friend. Mostly a business friend, but a friend nonetheless.

A gleam entered Jacob's eyes. "Perhaps you don't know this, but I know your brother, Aidan McNamara."

I nodded and swallowed. "Right. I knew that, but we've never met."

"I wasn't planning to kidnap you, if that's what you're wondering. As it stands, since the room is on his credit card, either you get out of there or he could kick you out. I figured you might want to keep your pride intact."

"Why did you help?"

"I happened to be walking by and overheard him. When I realized who you were, I decided to step in. You didn't deserve to be treated like that. I hate assholes."

"Oh," came my brilliant answer.

I couldn't seem to think straight when I was up close and personal with this man, not with my pulse leaping and heat prickling over my skin. "I suppose you're right about the room," I finally said. "I'm not really in a position to get another room though."

"I have a suite. There are two bedrooms," he said simply. "If you don't trust me, call Aidan."

Regardless of what my common sense might have thought, my gut told me I could trust Jacob. "Floor fifteen. Are you...?"

He shook his head. "No need to ask if I'm sure. It's really not a problem."

With Jacob's steady presence alongside me, I returned to the room and gathered my things. When I hesitated by the door, uncertain what to do with the key card, Jacob said, "I'll call down to the desk. Leave it here on the dresser."

In a matter of minutes, he had whisked me down a long hallway to a set of elevators I didn't know existed. Then, we were on the top floor, and he led me through a private entrance into his hotel suite. I felt as if I were living another life. Like a princess whisked away to a tower.

It was beautiful, of course. The entryway

was tiled in marble. Stepping beyond that into the living room, my heels were nearly silent on the plush carpet. The expansive space had floor-to-ceiling windows looking out over Las Vegas—Sin City glittering in the desert. Beyond the lights, there was nothing but blackness in the distance.

There was a fully outfitted kitchen, along with an office, the master bedroom, and another bedroom, which was still three times the size of the room I'd had many floors below. After I set my single suitcase down in front of the dresser, I wondered what to do next. I'd been out of my element to begin with in coming to Las Vegas on my own. It wasn't as if I hadn't lived in cities. I'd lived in both San Francisco and Seattle. Yet, a high-end hotel suite in Las Vegas, a city with its own heartbeat, had knocked me off balance.

Running into Wayne hadn't helped matters. I had no illusions about him. I didn't miss Wayne. In fact, I was relieved. I was glad I found out sooner rather than later just what kind of man he was.

But, I had my pride, and now I was in a virtual stranger's hotel suite. I might trust Jacob not to do anything insane, but I didn't know the social rules for this situation.

At all.

Chapter Two

ELLIE

Seeing as it was Las Vegas, I'd dressed up a bit tonight. I wore a cotton skirt that fit snugly around my hips and flared in a twirl at my knees. A pair of strappy, heeled sandals were on my feet with my toenails painted bright red. Atop my skirt, I wore a loose silky white blouse that felt comfortable and glamorous at once.

Taking a deep breath and marshaling my courage, I returned to the living room to find Jacob sipping on a drink. When the light caught on his glass from above, I guessed it to be whiskey. Probably the most expensive kind you could find.

"Were you planning to gamble while you

were here?" he asked as I approached him across the room.

The sound of my low, kitten heels clicked as I walked across the marble before going quiet on the plush carpet. He stood beside a bar that ran along the far wall.

"What would you like to drink?" he asked when I reached him.

"Well, it *is* Vegas, after all. Gambling is a requirement. And whatever you're having is fine."

"Would you like to know what I'm having?" he countered, a teasing glint entering his gaze.

My body could *not* seem to be normal around Jacob Taylor. My belly did a few flips and sparks flew through me.

I imagined he had this effect on every woman. It was a bit annoying. Men didn't usually get to me, not like this. I chalked it up to being completely out of my element, and rattled even more by Wayne showing up and being more of an asshole than he'd already been.

"I'm guessing that's whiskey," I finally replied.

I could smell the rich, woodsy scent of it, just barely.

This time, Jacob smiled. The smile unfurled slowly, from one corner of his mouth to the other, and sent my pulse into the stratosphere.

Without a word, he turned and set his glass down, quickly filling one for me and handing it over. I took a few sips, savoring the rich flavor and the burn of it on my tongue. I could use the liquid courage just now. Although it was past midnight, this was Vegas, and I knew the night was just beginning.

Jacob seemed relaxed, leaning his hand against the edge of the bar and watching me quietly. "Shall we go out then?"

"You mean, you and me?"

His eyes were assessing. I felt as if he were trying to read something in me. I felt far too exposed, sensing he could pick up on how off-kilter I was.

"What other 'we' would there be in this room?" he countered.

I laughed softly before gulping the rest of my whiskey, perhaps too quickly.

"Why not? I came to Vegas, and I've never been here. I might as well do it right."

Jacob nodded, seeming pleased with my answer. "I'll make sure of it. I hope you don't mind, but I texted Aidan and let him know you were with me."

I did mind. "Whatever for? My brother is certainly not my keeper."

"Precisely what he said you would say. I figured he would want to know you were okay."

I stared at Jacob and gave my head a shake. "You're a bit presumptuous, aren't you?"

"So I've been told," he replied smoothly, before he drained his whiskey and set the empty glass on the bar.

He seemed entirely unperturbed at my frustration toward him, turning smoothly and gliding his hand down my spine in a heated pass. Butterflies spun in my belly, and my sex clenched. Somehow, the anger mingling with this disconcerting desire had my body feeling crazy.

"Do you have a gambling preference?" he asked as we stepped into the elevator.

"Blackjack."

He didn't reply, he simply tapped the button on the elevator. Without a sound, it began moving rapidly. In a flash, he was standing in front of me. He leaned one hand on the wall behind me, his presence suddenly overwhelming. His scent hit my nostrils, crisp and musky, an overtly masculine scent. I wanted to burrow into him.

"For what it's worth, I'm a selfish man too," he said, the gravelly sound of his voice sending a prickle down my spine.

I was confused. "Excuse me?"

"Well, I *did* overhear your ex being an asshole, but I overheard because I was on my way over to invite you to dinner. Because you're fucking beautiful."

My mind went blank. Before I knew it, he dipped his head and brushed his lips across mine, the contact so electric my entire body vibrated with its force.

My brain tried to fire off a rational thought, but all reason was swept away in the melting heat of Jacob's exploratory kiss. Another brush of his lips across mine. There was no hurry, no intense, demanding kiss.

He nipped at my bottom lip, dusted kisses on each corner of my mouth, and swiped his tongue across the seam. Heat flooded my body and spun through my veins like sparks of fire. When his tongue swept into my mouth, I didn't even hesitate, sighing and inviting him in with a gasp.

In a distant corner of my mind, I was quite startled. When Jacob stepped closer, my hand slid up to cup his nape, his hair silky against my fingers, and I arched into him.

This kiss was everything—delicious, decadent, and the hottest kiss I'd ever had. Maybe it was because he surprised me. Maybe it was because he was about the most handsome man I'd ever seen. Maybe it was because my pride was still stinging a bit from my encounter with Wayne.

None of it mattered, nothing except for the feel of Jacob's mouth over mine—a slow, sensual tease unraveling me inside and leaving me hot and breathless, bordering on needy.

I didn't even notice the elevator stopping. I heard the sound of the casino spilling into my awareness when the doors whispered open. Jacob gentled our kiss slowly. As he drew away, his gaze held mine for a few beats. I felt stripped bare, as if he could see right into me, and it rattled me. This wasn't the kind of thing I did, kissing men I barely knew in elevators. Yet, I was entirely out of my element here in Las Vegas, roaming casinos alone.

I tried to speak, but my voice was lost in a rasp. Clearing my throat, I attempted again, this time succeeding. "What was that for?"

Jacob was quiet, and I sensed he was considering his response carefully. "I wanted to kiss you," he said simply.

I didn't know what to say to that, so I said, "Oh."

Jacob turned, his hand sliding down my back and guiding me as it rested in the dip at the base of my spine. His touch felt like a brand, the heat of it warming me straight through.

It was now going on one a.m., and it felt as if the night was just beginning. And not just because I'd had a crazy kiss in an elevator with an insanely handsome man. The pulse of Las Vegas spun me into its storm of glitter and lights and energy. I couldn't help but ride the waves.

Chapter Three

JACOB

Ellie McNamara was, simply put, stunning. With her glossy black hair, bright hazel eyes, and body of lush curves, it was a miracle she was here alone. I'd seen her only once before at a fundraiser with her brother. But she was with her boyfriend then, the fucking idiot.

I hadn't known what a jerk he was at the time. I don't know how I would've known. While her brother was a friend, it was mostly in the business sense. Calling Aidan up to check on his little sister wasn't exactly on my radar.

I'd been seated at a bar set back from the crowd and walkways in the casino when I saw Ellie from a distance, walking by herself and, frankly, looking a little lost.

Las Vegas could make anyone feel lost. It was a wild place. I didn't come here often myself, but I was here on business. I finished my drink and headed in her direction, and my timing couldn't have been better. I heard most of her interaction with her ex.

Aside from the fact that I wanted Ellie for myself, I also hated that he cheated on her. I'd been on the receiving end of cheating in my last so-called relationship. A number of problems were associated with being wealthy. There were plenty of women who wanted me, but very few who wanted me for anything other than the social status and the money that came with me.

I'd always been a rather skeptical person, yet my skepticism shifted to cynicism after I made a fortune when I wasn't even after the money. I wasn't looking for much from Ellie. I wouldn't take advantage of her, but I sure as hell wouldn't pass up the opportunity to kiss her. Or more, if she allowed it.

Humiliating her ex and the woman who appeared to know Ellie was my pleasure. I had gladly taken the opportunity they handed to me. I hadn't meant to offer up my suite, but I wasn't about to let her ex call the shots on his credit card. If she insisted, I would get her another room.

As it was, I was going to show her Las Vegas tonight. If she let me. I was a little thrown by the depth of lust that bolted through me the moment I was close to her, but I would manage it. Kissing her was like diving into a fire of heaven and hell. Heaven, because it felt so damn good. Hell, because she was so damn tempting, I could hardly bear it. I didn't like to feel out of control.

"Have you had dinner?" I asked as we rounded a corner in the hallway that led us away from the private elevator bank.

Ellie glanced up, her gaze catching mine. Her eyes were incredible. I hadn't seen them up close until tonight. Layers of green, gold, and nutmeg swirled together into a kaleidoscope of hazel.

"It's morning," she replied, her voice slightly husky, the sound of it alone sending a lash on the whip of lust, striking me.

I grinned. "It is, but it's Las Vegas, and time takes on its own meaning here. Let me rephrase. Are you hungry? And what shall we call your meal?"

Ellie returned my grin, and I was far too pleased. I shouldn't care whether or not she smiled, but I felt like a randy boy around her. There was an innocence to her, a refreshing, wholesome sultriness.

"I *am* hungry. Take me somewhere where they serve everything, so I can decide."

"Your wish is my command," I replied, sliding my hand from the center of her back to curl around her hip and savoring the soft give of her flesh under my fingers.

Ellie elicited a sense of possessiveness, and I didn't quite understand why. I barely knew her. None of it made sense, but I didn't give a damn. Not tonight.

I took her to a restaurant that served everything, as she requested. They had all meals available twenty-four hours a day. As I said, time took on its own meaning here in Vegas.

It was near impossible to find anything other than a nice restaurant in this part of Las Vegas. In my younger days, before I had money, I would've searched out an off-the-wall dive. That still would've been my preference now, but I had my reasons for queuing to the lines drawn by money. More than anything, I valued my privacy, and I would get it at a place like this.

After the hostess escorted us to a circular booth tucked into a corner, Ellie smiled over at me. I wanted to slide my arm around the curve of the table and tug her into my lap.

"Well, this is nice," she said as she glanced around.

Unlike many of the spaces in the casinos in Las Vegas, by some miracle, this place had stolen a little quiet. Although, I supposed it wasn't a miracle. It was a miracle wrought by carpeting, drapes, and doors that held the almost constant cacophony of noise in Las Vegas at bay.

Considering this place was housed in the casino attached to the same hotel where I frequently stayed, I had discovered it one morning. I often came here to work because of its quiet.

"It *is* nice. The food is good, and it's mostly quiet," I replied.

As if conjured by my words, a waiter appeared dressed in crisp black slacks and a starched white shirt. He looked to Ellie first. "Welcome. Would you like anything to drink?"

"I'll take a whiskey on the rocks, please." She glanced to me after she responded, and I had a hard time focusing on her question. Her mouth was nearly perfect. Thick, plush lips, glistening and still a little puffy from our kiss in the elevator.

"Mr. Taylor," he said with an inclination of his head. "What can I get for you?"

I forced myself to look away from Ellie. "I'll take the same."

With another nod, he added, "Please take a look at the menus. I'll be back with your drinks shortly."

He turned away, and I brought my attention back to Ellie. She didn't wear makeup. At all. She glowed, as if lit from within.

"So, what brings you to Las Vegas?" I asked.

"Well, I'm sure you could deduce from my conversation with Wayne that we had planned a trip here. That was before I came across a text from my former friend, Cheryl, on his phone," she explained with a twist of her lips and a shadow chasing across her features.

"As we've established, Wayne is a fucking idiot," I said flatly.

Ellie shrugged. "It's for the best, but it still sucks, you know?"

"I do know. I've been burned myself. It's quite enlightening."

She brushed the silky fall of her hair off her shoulder and angled her head to the side. "You?"

"Yes. Me."

"That's crazy. I mean, you're rich, powerful, and handsome. I would think women would be falling all over themselves for you," she said, so earnestly I couldn't help but laugh.

"Comments on looks aside, I get your point, but people often go for the superficial."

"You heard my sob story. Tell me yours," she said, leaning back just as our waiter arrived with our drinks.

"Do you need a few minutes?" he asked politely, glancing from Ellie to me after he served our drinks.

"I haven't even looked at the menu yet. You're so efficient. Give us a few minutes. Unless you're ready," she added with an arch of a brow in my direction.

"A few minutes would be nice."

Ellie dutifully opened her menu as the waiter smiled politely and turned away. "Oh my God, you weren't kidding! They have everything. There are three pages for each meal—breakfast, lunch, and dinner. You're not paying," she said, narrowing her eyes in my direction.

"Don't even argue about it with me. It doesn't need to be a point of pride. I wasn't always wealthy. Your brother would kill me if I let you rack up a credit card bill for the sake of a meal I can easily cover."

Two red spots appeared on Ellie's cheeks. I could practically visualize the thoughts careening around her mind.

After a moment, she rolled her eyes. "Fine. It would be a point of pride, and I'm stubborn, but I'm not stupid. Thank you," she said with a twist of her mouth.

Chapter Four

JACOB

I didn't know what the hell it was about this woman, but she got to me. She had a straight line to the heartbeat of lust in my body. I had definitely thought her beautiful back when I first saw her, but she was taken, so I kept my distance. A glimpse of someone also doesn't give you much.

But this? Seeing her steely pride and the vulnerability so close to the surface, it caught me and drew me in. About five years ago, my life exploded. My little sister was killed by her ex who had stalked her. He tracked her down through one of those social media apps. On the heels of that, I dedicated my knowledge of computer coding and hacking to create software and apps that could shut down all those online tentacles that created openings for unsavory people to exploit.

Although I had very personal reasons for the work I did, my timing was unintentionally perfect. Social media giants were faced with increasing calls for managing privacy. That was how I met Ellie's brother. He ran a high-end security company based in Seattle and offered to do some beta testing when I ran into him at a conference.

I'd gone from a young man a few years out of college, grieving the loss of my sister, and furious about it, to wealthy beyond anything I could've imagined. A side effect was far more attention was paid to my private life than I ever wanted. I tried not to get jaded, but it was damn near impossible.

Ellie was right, women did chase me, or rather the idea of me. My last girlfriend screwed around on me—quite a bit, in fact.

What it was about Ellie that got to me, I couldn't say. She was genuine in a way that was rare these days. I knew nothing but a sketch of her life. Aidan had only told me their parents had passed away, and she was an artist.

"I'm going to have the biscuits and gravy," she announced out of the blue, effectively bringing my attention to the moment.

"With whiskey?" I asked, fighting a grin.

"Yes, I love biscuits and gravy. It's delicious and mild. It should taste just fine with the whiskey," she said with a laugh. "When do people sleep here anyway?"

I shrugged. "I suppose whenever. Truth is, I don't usually gamble, but tonight, I was attending a scheduled game of poker. It's not that common for me to be up this late either."

She sipped her whiskey and eyed me. "What are you having?" she asked, shifting the topic.

"Now that you mention it, biscuits and gravy sounds delicious."

"I doubt it's gourmet," she commented with a sly grin.

"Gourmet or not, I'm confident it will be delicious. Nothing here has failed me before," I said, just as the waiter arrived.

After we ordered, he glanced between us. "Anything else?"

Ellie shook her head. At my nod, he turned away, assuring us our food would be out promptly.

Ellie looped the conversation back to our earlier interruption. "So, back to you, what's your sob story?"

"I wouldn't call it a sob story, more a learning experience."

Sipping her whiskey, she circled her hand in the air, indicating I should continue.

"It's a trite story. Back when my business first took off, things were crazy. I had more money than I knew what to do with it, and more attention than I cared to manage. But I'm a man, and I'll admit, I didn't mind some of the perks. I wasn't jaded at first. It didn't take long. I dated a woman who I thought was exclusive with me. Turned out, she wasn't. In fact, she was far from exclusive. Unlike you, it didn't involve a friend of mine, but rather a business acquaintance. I learned my lesson. Quite well. She wanted my money and the cachet of being with me, but she certainly didn't want anything serious."

"How was that a lesson?" Ellie asked.

"The lesson was to remember expectations."

"What do you mean?"

"Most people don't want me for me. They want the package, the superficial benefits. So, I leave it at that. While I think Wayne was an idiot, you don't need to worry that I want something serious from you."

Ellie was quiet, and for just a second, the desolation in her eyes sent a chill through me. But my heart was all but encased in ice. I knew somehow whatever I said had hurt her. I certainly hadn't meant to, and I felt it fiercely. On the heels of that icy sensation was a burning need to make it right.

"I don't suppose that came out the way I meant it," I said slowly.

Ellie took a swallow of her whiskey and shook her head. "I don't know how you meant it, but I don't have any expectations."

As I sat there staring at her, it felt as if a line of electricity sizzled in the air between us. I certainly wished I could take my words back. And that didn't make a lick of sense.

It chafed at me to hear Ellie say she had no expectations. I could tolerate my own bitterness and cynicism about life, but not hers.

My thoughts began to roll down the track where I told myself she deserved to have someone—someone who could worship that hint of innocence she carried with her. With the wholesome sultriness that came so naturally to her, I found it a damn miracle another man hadn't already staked his claim. Though, most definitely not her asshole ex.

The problem with this line of thinking was that the moment my mind began following it, a fierce sense of possessiveness took hold. I might not have any expectations, but I didn't want anyone else to have Ellie. I was quite certain—crazy as it was—that only *I* could appreciate her for the woman she was. Which was beyond crazy. It was insane.

I was so unsettled with my reaction I gulped the rest of my whiskey in one swallow. Ellie watched me quietly, something flickering in her gaze. She looked away, her eyes scanning the restaurant curiously.

Our waiter conveniently arrived, likely having noticed my drink was empty. I ordered another and forced my mind to be more disciplined. I might want Ellie and I might've been reckless enough to kiss her in the elevator, but my life had no room for anything beyond casual.

The night—or rather, the morning, if you prefer to be exact—carried on. We had our meal, and I swept her off with me to the promised game of blackjack. She was surprisingly good and teased me with tales of how she learned. Apparently, her father had loved to gamble for fun and taught her and Aidan to play when they were young. She freely admitted she rarely gambled for money. She refused to let me bet on her behalf and proceeded to win a tidy sum of money, quitting while she was well ahead.

Las Vegas spun its magic. Whenever I

was here, which wasn't too often, it was easy to feel as though you were suspended in time —a time of glitter when night and day turned upside down.

Despite the state of my body, and my cock's rather persistent protest, I determined I needed to keep my distance from the sweet and sultry Ellie.

I refrained from any more drinks after those first two, although she had a few more as the night wore on and was quite tipsy when I escorted her back to the room. She was just tipsy enough I could easily ratio-nalize I would be taking advantage if I dared to kiss her again. That was my excuse, not my body's intense reaction to her and the under-lying fear that somehow, she could rattle the cage I had built around my heart.

It was probably four in the morning, or thereabouts, when she turned in the doorway of her bedroom in the suite, leaning her shoulder against the doorframe. She held her sandals in her hand with her fingers looped through the straps. My eyes landed on her bright red toenails, the splash of color fitting. Her dark hair was tousled from brushing it out of the way a few too many times as we had meandered through the crowded casinos.

The night ended when she asked me to

take one more walk just so she could see everything. Her cheeks were flushed and her eyes snagged mine. I wanted to touch her so fucking badly. My eyes dipped down, taking in the curve of her hips, the way her blouse fell open slightly, offering me a tease of lace barely peeking out past where her blouse came together in the center.

"Thank you for tonight, Jacob," she said softly, her voice raspy from being surrounded by smoke and drinking all night.

My cock protested again, pressing against my zipper. I willfully ignored it and inclined my head. "You're quite welcome. Thank you for the company. Las Vegas is a city better enjoyed with someone else."

She smiled and a hint of bitterness dashed across her face. I knew she was recalling precisely why she was here. Her idiot ex and the trip they were supposed to take together.

"Good night," she said, roughly pushing away from the door and turning.

The door closed softly behind her with a *click* and I stared at it, seriously contemplating for a few seconds the idea of walking right over, opening that door, and persuading her to share my bed.

That was plain crazy.

Chapter Five

JACOB

I rose mid-morning after a solid five hours of sleep. I figured Ellie would still be asleep. After a quick check, merely peeking into her bedroom to see she was sound asleep, I left a note on the counter that I would be working for the day. I also texted her phone with my number.

I had several meetings today. The sole reason I was in Las Vegas was to meet with investors and shore up some collaborative partnerships for my software and smartphone applications. There was a conference here on tech security, which made it quite convenient for me to meet with multiple business partners in one location, rather than scattered across the country.

Being based in Seattle gave me a little breathing room from the hub of Silicon Valley. I preferred it that way, if only because it prevented me from being pressured by irrational trends that could drive unwise business decisions.

Walking to one of my meetings at a restaurant a few hotels down from where I was staying, it occurred to me Ellie and I both lived in Seattle. It wasn't as if I hadn't known that fact before. Yet, now that I'd had more than a glimpse of her, now that I had experienced her answering desire, and now that my own body had made its preferences astonishingly clear, the fact that Ellie and I could be something more than a one-off, one- night stand in Las Vegas struck me at my core, chinking the armor of my cynicism.

I literally shook my head in an effort to kick her out of my mind.

"That bad to see me?" Darren Greene's voice reached me.

Following the sound, I looked to my right to see him already seated at a booth in the restaurant. It barely registered for me that I had paused beside the hostess who directed me this way.

"Oh no, just puzzling over some accounting details," I said, the lie rolling smoothly off my tongue.

Darren owned a security business right here in Las Vegas. He was also one of the hosts for this conference. I slipped into the booth across from him and smiled. "How are you this morning?"

"Quite well, but then, unlike most everyone visiting here, I had a full night's sleep," he replied, his brown eyes catching mine.

I chuckled, reaching for the coffee the waitress had poured as I was sitting down. "So true. I got a full five hours though."

I knew Darren from visiting here before. Las Vegas might be one of the most profitable cities to be handling security, and Darren had his thumb on the pulse of the entire city.

He contracted for some of the most high-end casinos and hotels in town and leveraged those relationships for worldwide coordination in the security field. He and Aidan were friends as well. Aidan had no interest in expanding his business, although he occasionally handled national and international jobs when it suited him.

After a sip of my coffee, I glanced over. "Is anyone else meeting us?"

"Oh no. I wanted to pitch this to you first. I want to integrate your software into all of my systems here in Las Vegas. We can run it as a pilot and see how it goes. As it is right now, people either have your app on their phones, or you're doing it for security companies, if I understand correctly, right?"

"Yes. So far, that's how we've done it. I'm not sure how what you're proposing would be different."

Darren nodded, brushing a loose lock of his brown hair back from his forehead. "This way, we can link it into every system—banking and whatnot. Privacy is becoming more and more of an issue. I find our guys are spending a ton of time chasing down potential weak points into various secure systems. I'd like to centralize it without increasing risk. It'll be a closed system for each hotel."

His comments showed he had anticipated my protest about centralizing it. I chuckled before taking another sip of my coffee. "Fair enough. I was going to say, as soon as it's tapped into anything that's open source, it puts my system at risk. But if each system stays closed, that would mitigate it. If I'm going to do this with anyone, I would do it with you."

Darren flashed a quick grin.

"Let's hash out how to deal with it, but I've got to look at the coding for every single system if I'm gonna feel comfortable with this."

Darren knew me well and had considered every contingency. After we finished breakfast, we left to go to his offices to work. Between shared projects and conference business, we had plenty to keep us busy. I ignored the tiny pull to come up with some excuse to return to my hotel to check on something. But I had no excuse, none whatsoever. I just wanted to see Ellie.

Fortunately, or so I thought at first, I had enough to focus on that Ellie only intruded on my thoughts periodically. By the time early evening rolled around and the lights began coming on in Vegas, I glanced at my watch and saw it was 5:45 p.m. I knew Ellie was here for three more days. I didn't want to leave her to her own devices at night. I usually wouldn't worry much about someone else's plan, but there was that tug. I couldn't stop thinking about that reckless kiss. I assured myself I had nothing but noble intentions.

Darren dispatched me back to my hotel with his car service, and I arrived a few minutes after six. I was weaving through the crowded casino to get to the private bank of elevators at the back when everything went black.

By black, I mean completely dark. Every single light went out. There was a moment of startled silence, and you could feel the room almost collectively holding its breath. After a moment, a few emergency lights came on, indicating where the exits were. A glance at the windows gave me nothing more than the last lingering rays of the sun above the skyline in the distance.

An urgency struck me. I needed to find Ellie. *Now*. When nothing changed and no lights came back on, people began to pull out their phones and frantically check. Battery power would last us a bit if this was anything other than a blip.

I kept expecting the generators to kick in, but they didn't. Two words beat a staccato tempo in my brain. *Find Ellie*.

Chapter Six

ELLIE

I stood in the middle of a crowded walkway in the casino, the room abruptly pitch-black. Everyone froze. I could feel the collective confusion and the weighted expectation that, surely, the lights would come back on.

They didn't. After a moment of silence, voices picked up around me, murmurs running through the room. People were checking their phones. When I glanced to my screen, there was no reception whatsoever.

I told myself to stay calm. Generators would kick in, and everything would carry on as usual. Whatever had caused the power to blink out would be resolved.

Something felt off. My gut pinged with

anxiety. After everyone had frozen for a moment, people began to move, following the dim lighting of the emergency exit signs. My anxiety ramped up a few more notches. I was alone in an endless maze of interconnected hotels and casinos surrounded by strangers. I knew a whopping total of three people in this city, two of whom I didn't care to see at all.

I frantically tapped at my phone, seeing the lack of signal and wishing it away. I could still read the text Jacob had sent me this morning.

Ellie, I have meetings most of the day. I'll be back early this evening. I hope we can have dinner again.

I desperately wanted to reply and ask him where he was. I had no idea how to find him. The sun had dipped below the horizon within the last hour. Whatever glimmers of light were left outside, I couldn't tell. The thousands of people crowding the Las Vegas casinos had been plunged into darkness.

The murmured voices rose in volume, people calling out questions, while I stayed frozen where I was. I suddenly wished I had more nerve last night. As I had stood in the bedroom door looking at Jacob, so damn handsome it almost hurt to look at him, I wanted to walk up to him and get another one of his kisses. I wanted *far* more than kisses.

But I hadn't had the nerve. My confidence had taken quite a hit last year—thanks to Wayne and Cheryl. If you were wondering, it's bad enough when someone cheats on you. It's far worse when it's with one of your friends. It's like the layers of trust are violated on a deeper level, adding a stinging bonus point to the betrayal.

In the darkness, I lost my bearings and my sense of which way to go to get back to the hotel suite. In this casino, I was on a ground floor. Jacob's suite was high in the sky. I would have to climb stairs in the darkness to get there, likely joined by hordes of strangers.

I began moving, deliberately and cautiously, in the direction where I thought I needed to go. In Las Vegas, with its maze of interconnected buildings, it would not be difficult to get lost, even with all the lights on. In the darkness, with the murmur of panic running amongst the crowds of people, it was definitely a shade more difficult.

I beat back my anxiety. I felt unsteady and confused and something felt off. It was one thing to lose power, yet another for the generators to fail, and yet another for all cell reception to go out.

I wished Jacob were right here with me. He had a strong, protective presence like my brother. Well, it was quite a bit different, seeing as I felt nothing but brotherly affection for Aidan, while Jacob had me hot and bothered with nothing more than a look. I had just about talked myself into a fling with him last night, but then, I wasn't really a fling kind of girl.

Bodies bumped into me, and it felt as if I was in a cave. What appeared to be a convenience when the power was working felt like a prison when it wasn't, with all the hallways and only a few windows looking outward. A hand squeezed my ass, and I swatted it away, a flash of anger piercing me.

I sternly told myself I would just keep walking. I would find the right place, and I would go up however many stairs I had to climb. No matter what, I had faith Jacob would find me. I just didn't know quite where he was right now.

A riff of fear chased down my spine, and I told myself I was overreacting. The lights would come back on in any minute. All the while, I kept putting one foot in front of the other.

I reached an area that intercepted with a hallway with windows to the outside. I was stunned when I glanced over my shoulder to see the darkness stretching out. The moon was rising above the mountains that sat at a distance from Las Vegas across the desert. That light was a sharp contrast to the sheer absence of it everywhere else. The famous excess and hedonism of Las Vegas in the desert was temporarily offline.

From the streets outside, I heard voices shouting. I paused, taking a minute to study the mountains. I'd looked at them this morning and knew the orientation of where one taller peak lined up with the hotel where I was staying with Jacob.

A shaft of relief pierced me when I identified it under the silver glow of the moon.

I didn't have the virtue of many landmarks to use, but I could guess I needed to pass through one more building based on where I thought the mountain peak was.

I kept walking, along with many others. With nothing but the dim glow of emergency exit lights, there were a few panicky voices and a hum of distress running through the crowd. I kept moving, with more bodies bumping into me, and another hand colliding with my hip, although this one felt more accidental than purposeful.

By the time I reached what I thought was the juncture to the right hotel, my heart was pounding, and there was a sheen of sweat on my skin. People kept calling out to staff because they were everywhere, and no one knew anything.

I realized I knew where the bank of elevators was, but not the stairs. I was still largely blind from the darkness in the crowd, although a few people were using lights from their phones. I didn't dare because I didn't want the battery to die too soon. At this rate, my gut was telling me we weren't going to get power soon.

I figured I'd find my way to the elevators and perhaps I could see signs to the stairs from there. Moments later, I got there to find a line and suddenly wanted to cry. The idea of climbing that many stairs seemed utterly exhausting.

Suddenly, I felt a hand press between my shoulder blades. "Ellie." I recognized Jacob's voice instantly. In sheer relief, I turned into him. He pulled me into his embrace, strong and sheltering.

I wasn't prone to having meltdowns. I generally took things in stride. But I was rattled and disoriented by the situation. I realized how tightly I was coiled inside the moment he held me close. I buried my face in his chest and almost burst into tears.

I took several shuddering breaths, breathing in his crisp, masculine scent. Regardless of the situation, my body responded to the feel of him and his scent wrapping around me. His hand circled on my back as he murmured wordlessly into my hair. When I thought I had it together and wouldn't cry, I lifted my head, barely able to make out his features in the darkness.

"I'm so glad you found me," I whispered.

"I don't know if you can be as glad as I am." His voice was somber and taut with constrained concern.

"Do you know what happened?"

"No idea. Something's wrong because the generators should've come on, and they haven't. There's no cell reception either."

"I know. I was going to text and ask you where you were."

"I'm right here now," he said, this time his voice a little more relaxed.

"Should we try to get up to the room?"

"I'm not sure. On the one hand, if we have any chance of picking up a signal, at that elevation, our chances would be better.

On the other, that's a lot of stairs to climb. And if the power doesn't come back on, I'm not so sure it's a smart choice, seeing as we probably can't get into our room without breaking down the door since it's activated by a key card."

I was quiet, absorbing the implications of what he said. I didn't know what the best thing to do was, but I certainly didn't want to stay down here amongst everyone, feeling slightly panicked.

"Do we have any other options?"

"Do you have your purse?" he asked.

"Of course. Is there anything important you need from the room?"

I felt him shake his head. "I travel light. I only have clothes and my laptop. Aside from my clothes, everything else is right here," he explained, lifting a slender, secured briefcase. "I have a friend who lives here in Las Vegas. I won't be able to get word to him, but he runs security for many of the casinos here. I know he has offices and an apartment on the bottom floor across the street. We can go there. Whether he's there or not, I know he won't care if we are. I'll feel better about that until we know what's going on. We have a long way to go if we try to go upstairs."

"Let's go then," I said.

We were speaking quietly, low enough
not to be heard by those around us. When I
paused, I could hear similar conversations
around us. Most of the ground floors of the
casinos were occupied with businesses. It
was a sheer stroke of luck Jacob had a
friend who had space on the lower floor
nearby.

He moved swiftly, startling me when he
dipped his head and brushed his lips against
mine. I didn't know what he meant it to be,
but I leaned into his kiss, needing the contact. It was electric—the feel of his mouth
searing hot before he drew back.

"Okay, let's go," he said quickly. He held
his briefcase tightly in one hand with his
other hand curled around my hip. With a
gentle pressure, he guided me through the
crowds and down a single flight of stairs
where we exited onto the street. It was just as
crowded out here as it was inside, with
people milling about and speculating about
what had happened.

Jacob was single-minded, guiding me with
a firm press through the crowds. Although
my anxiety eased slightly once I encountered
Jacob, my heart was still pounding and a
sense of unease rippled through me. The
coaxing pressure of his hand kept moving me

forward with him as we made our way through the crowd.

I savored the sense of protectiveness cloaked around us with his presence. I didn't have a clear sense of time, but I knew we hadn't gone far. It felt like it took longer than it should've, but then, we were moving in the shadowy, smudgy darkness with people all around as the collective concern multiplied.

"Right here," he murmured, leaning down toward my ear as he guided us to a doorway.

Although there were people all around us, everyone appeared to be going somewhere. Jacob stopped right in front of what appeared to be a service entrance, and we stood for several minutes. He leaned down again, speaking into my ear, the gruff sound of his voice sending a prickle of goose bumps over my skin.

"Gonna wait a few minutes before we go in. I don't want to draw attention."

He had one hand resting against the hard surface of the building wall, and the other still curled around my waist, pulling me into the shelter of his embrace.

"How are we going to get in?" I asked, keeping my voice low.

"It's run remotely. I'm assuming everything has failed because of the power outage. I have a backup key."

"You do?"

I could feel his lips curve against the side of my neck from where he was bent low, his cheek brushing against mine. "I do. Darren's a good friend, and we've worked together on a number of projects. That's who I met with today. I'll get us in here, and we'll figure it out from there."

Jacob stayed quiet, lifting his head, his alert gaze scanning the area around us. My eyes had adjusted to the darkness, and I could see the press of people nearby on the sidewalks. During a moment when someone was calling from across the street and giving an update on the generator situation for a hotel, Jacob swiftly opened the door and had us inside in a matter of seconds.

Unlike everywhere else we'd been, this did not appear to be a casino hallway.

The voices from outside were muted in here.

Jacob led me down a hallway as my eyes adjusted to the deeper darkness in this area. Stopping in front of a door, he knocked sharply, with his other arm still wrapped around my waist. As unsettled as I felt given our current situation, I was somehow certain that everything would be fine as long as I stayed with Jacob.

Several quiet beats passed, and Jacob knocked again, calling softly, "Darren. If you're in there, it's Jacob."

After another moment, I heard footsteps and the door opened. Jacob escorted us in quickly and closed the door, locking it behind him.

Chapter Seven

ELLIE

"This is Ellie McNamara," Jacob said quickly.

"Jacob, I hoped you had enough sense to come over here," a man said. I could barely make out the man until he held up his cell phone, tapping a button to illuminate the screen. "Still got plenty of battery power," he said with a smile, then looked at me. "You must be Aidan McNamara's sister."

"I am. How do you know Aidan?" I asked.

Darren flashed a smile. He was quite handsome. As best I could make out in the small light cast from his cell phone, he had sharp features, twinkling eyes, and dark hair flecked with silver.

"Darren Greene," he offered with a nod.

"I know your brother because I work in security too. Nice to meet you." He glanced back to Jacob. "Glad you found your way here. I'm thinking it's not good to be on the top floor of anywhere right now. Far as I can tell, everything is down except emergency lighting."

"Any idea why?" Jacob asked.

"Whatever it is, they sabotaged the generators too. Possibly a hacker, but I don't know. You got here just in time. I'm leaving to head home. Our condo's a few blocks away, but Sarah and Dee are there. You two can hang here as long as you need to."

"You sure?" Jacob asked.

"Absolutely. I came back here after our meeting to check on a few things before I went home. You can lock up behind me, and the place is yours. The offices are here, but there's a suite in the back. If this goes on through the night, there's a small kitchenette and a bed. Can't promise I've kept it too well-stocked, but you won't starve tonight," Darren said with a low chuckle. "You're welcome to come with me to my place."

Jacob shook his head. "Nah. You go be with your family. At least here, when the power comes on, if you don't mind, I'll use your systems to do a little digging."

Darren nodded. "Of course. I'm headed out." He clapped Jacob on the shoulder as he left and quickly slipped out the door, which Jacob bolted behind him.

Jacob's hand fell away from my waist during this exchange. I hadn't realized I missed the heat of his touch until I felt his palm between my shoulder blades again, sliding down my spine to rest in the curve of my lower back.

"Come on, no sense in staying here in the offices."

I was acutely aware of his warm touch as I walked with him down a hallway to another door. I considered how much I took light for granted. It felt as if I were absorbing every space in increments.

The office area had been a bit louder. When we stepped through the next door, my feet shifted from the *click* of hard tile to soft carpeting, my low heels sinking into it.

"It's been a while since I've been here," he murmured as his hand fell away from me.

"Why does he have this suite in his offices?" I asked, genuinely curious.

"This is where he started his security business, and he used to live here, handling everything on-site. That was before he got married."

"Oh. Well, that makes sense," I said. I stood there, uncertain what to do. We were alone in the darkness with nothing to distract us.

"Do you need anything to drink?" he asked, as I heard his footfalls shift from the muted sound on the carpet to a louder step on what I presumed was tile.

"Do you think he has water?" I asked, following the sound of Jacob's voice across the room, my eyes gradually adjusting to the level of darkness in here.

"I'm sure he has water. In fact, there's a water cooler right here."

Jacob opened a cabinet, pulling out two glasses. "He's also got wine. And whiskey," he added with a chuckle.

"I'll just take the water for now."

With my eyes fully adjusted, I stepped to his side as he filled two glasses with water and handed one to me.

"This way to the couch." Jacob's hand rested against my hip as he angled us in another direction.

My eyes made out a sectional, and I sank down onto it with a sigh. Kicking my sandals off, I curled my feet under my knees and sipped my water. "This is weird," I finally said.

Jacob sat down beside me, and I felt more than saw him look in my direction. "That it is," he replied.

"So, you think it's on purpose?" I asked.

"That's my best guess since the generators aren't working."

I chewed the corner of my lip. I could finally see Jacob's eyes in the darkness. Desire chased through me. It felt out of place, but then, I supposed it wasn't, considering that one kiss last night in the elevator currently ranked as the hottest kiss I'd ever experienced. I imagined Jacob was quite accustomed to women wanting him. While my mind protested I would simply be lining up with all the rest, it didn't change the depth of my body's response to him.

"What should we do?" I heard myself asking. In the smudgy shades of darkness, I could feel the heat of his gaze on me. "Do you even remember what time it was when the power went off?"

"It was around six because that was about when I got back to the hotel and tried to find you."

I suppose I should've felt uncomfortable. I certainly didn't know Jacob very well. The only thing unsettling me in his presence was the background concern about what had caused the blackout. Well that, and the desire I couldn't seem to keep a lid on. It spun through my veins—a hot, liquid need. And here he was, a billionaire and so handsome, it almost hurt to look at him. For that, the darkness made me grateful. I didn't need to let my self-consciousness get the best of me.

I took a sip of my water and considered perhaps I should take him up on having some whiskey or wine. It might settle my nerves. I felt jumpy at his nearness and too needy for my own sanity.

I never thought much about how the distractions of modern life were simply that—distractions. In the quiet night, there was nothing to take my attention away.

"I meant to take you out another night on the town. I'm guessing that won't be the case tonight," he commented.

Glancing over and wrestling with the magnetic pull toward him, I made what was probably a reckless decision. For whatever reason, Jacob seemed to want me too, if his kiss in the elevator last night represented anything. In this city, so removed from my own life, and on this night, when all other distractions were gone for the moment, I might as well take something for myself.

Whether I should or not, I trusted Jacob.

I knew Aidan trusted him, so by extension, I did as well. Of course, I would have to extract his promise that Aidan would never know about this.

That is, if Jacob let me have my way.

Ever since my messy breakup with Wayne, Aidan had been more protective than usual. He was—with good reason, in my opinion—disgusted by Wayne's actions. But he was also angry with Cheryl. I didn't need my brother having any kind of opinion about me snatching one impulsive night for myself.

With my pulse humming along at high speed, I set my water down on the coffee table, having found it by feel when I came over to the sofa. Angling toward Jacob, I asked, "So, tell me, can you make me a promise?"

There was a weighted pause before he answered slowly, "I'd like to say yes, but I don't know what you're going to ask me to promise."

"Why did you kiss me last night?"

I felt his thigh against my knee as he moved slightly. The brushing touch sent a hot shiver through me.

"Because I wanted to," he said bluntly.

I felt as if I were watching myself from a distance. My confidence was coming in fitful starts. I knew what I felt between us, and I recognized it as pure desire. Yet, my confidence in general was rather banged up. Even though I could see Wayne for who he was and intellectually tell myself I deserved better, knowing that and believing it at my core was challenging.

My heart was pounding so hard I could feel the rush of blood in my ears. "Do you want more?" I asked, my voice raspy.

It showed how unsophisticated I was at this that I hadn't even expected to ask that question. It simply slipped out, almost forcefully, my words a little shaky.

There was another heavy silence. It felt almost electric, the way the air did right before a thunderstorm—loaded and waiting to unleash.

There were maybe inches between us where we sat on the couch. Jacob leaned forward, setting his glass of water on the table. The soft *clink* of the glass against what I assumed was a wooden surface was loud in the quiet room.

Leaning back, he angled to face me, lifting a hand and trailing his fingers through the ends of my hair where it fell down around my shoulders. The touch was subtle. He didn't even touch my skin, yet I felt it everywhere, sensation skittering through me like glittery sparks.

"Of course I want more, Ellie," he said, his tone low and intent.

"Then, let's have one night. But here's what I want you to promise. You can't tell Aidan about it."

If I thought the air felt electric before, now it was fairly vibrating. I wouldn't have been surprised to see sparks firing in the air between us.

Jacob was quiet long enough that doubts started bouncing around in my mind, little pings in the pulse of recklessness that had falsely inflated my confidence.

"I shouldn't have said anything," I said quickly, my words catching in my throat.

I leaned back, almost scrambling away from him on the couch, but he reached out, his hand catching my elbow and holding me still. "No, it's not that. It's not as if I would call Aidan and tell him anything. But if he were to ask me, I can't promise I would feel comfortable lying to him. I don't see why he would ask, but you never know."

I caught my bottom lip in my teeth, chewing it slightly. I wished it wasn't so dark, so I could see more than shadows and hints of Jacob's expression.

"Oh. I don't see what reason Aidan would have to ask you," I finally said.

"I suppose not," he replied quietly. "Whether it's sensible or not, I like you more than I should." A thrill shot through me at his words. Somehow, I desperately wanted to know if he felt the same desire I did.

Jacob was quiet for a few beats before he shifted closer to me, immediately erasing the distance I had created moments earlier. He was that kind of man who made you feel both overpowered and entirely protected, all at once.

With my personal life in shambles when it came to men, this desire was like a forbidden drink I couldn't resist. In fact, I wanted to gulp it down and get drunk on it. With everything spinning into this strange evening—with the power going out and unease an undercurrent under everything—losing myself in this almost seemed the safest thing to do.

"I can promise I certainly won't bring it up with him," Jacob said softly, his words falling into the darkness. Then, he laced his fingers in my hair as he slid his hand up to cup my nape. I meant to say something, but I didn't have a chance. I didn't care either.

His lips brushed across mine again, the

sensation electric with the subtle, teasing touch. He dusted kisses at each corner of my lips and then his tongue swept across the seam. I sighed. He fit his mouth over mine, my sigh getting lost in our kiss.

Chapter Eight

JACOB

Ellie tasted like honey and smelled like strawberries. Never in my life had I thought that subtle scent would turn me on, and yet, it was suddenly an aphrodisiac.

The subtly sweet smell tugged at me, pulling me deeper and deeper into the flames flickering around us. Ellie made me crazy. Her bold request that I make her a promise —bold, not because she preferred to keep her brother out of this, but because I sensed considering a night with a man like me wasn't something she did often. If ever.

That was intoxicating to me. I wasn't accustomed to a woman tugging at me like this with a desire that ran so deep it may be reckless.

Ellie sighed into our kiss as I dove into the warm sweetness of her mouth. Every sound was heightened by the silence around us. Cloaked in shadows and darkness, and alone amidst the rumble around us, the blackout made it feel as if everything we did was a moment out of time. It was a space where all rules were suspended. A space where whatever happened would remain sparkling and almost surreal.

Ellie's tongue slicked against mine. I shifted closer to her. Everywhere she touched me—her hand sliding up around my neck, her knee nudging against my thigh as she angled toward me, her lips moving under mine—every point was electric and sent sparks shooting through me.

With lust lashing at me, its force was so potent I felt driven, pulled directly into the undertow of it, the force of it undeniable. I felt rushed and didn't want to rush at all. I wanted to savor this.

Because Ellie was everything—her shyness wrapped up in her innate sultriness was beyond alluring. I wanted her with a ferocity that was entirely unfamiliar to me. I was accustomed to appreciating women. When it came to sex, I always made sure I took care of anyone I was with, controlling the tempo, the crescendo, and finding my own release only after that.

This experience of feeling caught up and tossed asunder by a desire so fierce I could barely keep hold of it was unsettling. And yet, it felt so damn good. The feel of her mouth against mine, the hint of what was to come with her breast pressing against my forearm. I needed her closer. *Now*.

Breaking free from her lips, I dusted kisses along her jawline and nipped at her earlobe. I savored the feel of her skin prickling with goose bumps under my lips as I trailed kisses over the downy skin of her neck, pausing at the wild beat of her pulse.

I tugged her closer, and she rose up on her knees and straddled me. She let out a ragged gasp when she settled over my hips with my arousal resting at the apex of her thighs. Just like last night, she was wearing a skirt, which rode up along her thighs.

I could feel the damp heat of her through the denim of my jeans. I loosened my hand caught in her hair and leaned back, looking at her in the silvery darkness. Having been in darkness for over an hour now, my eyes had adjusted well. Her hair fell in a tousle around her shoulders. I could feel the rapid rise and fall of her breath as her taut nipples pressed through the thin cotton of her blouse against my chest.

I wanted to rush, to tear her clothes off and feel every glorious inch of her against me. That pressing need, coiling tightly inside, battled with the desire to not miss a second of this, to unwrap her slowly like a present. Because I didn't know if I could bear more than one night with her. As it was, she threatened the foundation of my control, rattled me to my core, and made me want far more than I ever thought I would want.

Cynic, workaholic, a man who couldn't even be bothered to take advantage of the benefits of being wealthy—that's how most people who knew me described me. Except for my sister. Who I loved dearly and who was dead.

Ellie sliced right through that. My fierce need for her was like a river thawing after winter and running down a mountainside—its force undeterred, recklessly moving forward, breaking through ice and tossing everything in its path out of the way.

I didn't want to dwell on it. All I wanted was Ellie and to lose myself in her for this single, stolen night.

I slid a hand up her spine, levering her toward me and capturing her lips with mine again. She was so fucking responsive, her tongue darting out and tangling with mine. I loved how there was absolutely no artifice to her. Even when she was abandoning herself to pure lust, she still had that wholesome quality, making her so damn sexy I could hardly bear it.

I was under no illusions that she was innocent, like a virgin or some such nonsense. But the authenticity of the desire was laid bare between us and the way she threw herself into it was intoxicating. I wanted to eat her up, to taste every inch of her.

Her hips shifted over the hard ridge of my arousal, and I broke free from our kiss with a low growl, murmuring, "Slow down, sweetheart."

Ellie giggled and the sound itself was an arrow straight to my heart. Damn. This woman could make me lose my mind.

"Why?" she asked, a hint of her giggle still in her tone.

"Because this is too good," I said, my honesty shocking me. "You're delicious, and I want to make sure I taste every bite."

At that, I leaned forward, lightly grazing one of her nipples with my teeth. She gasped, the sound driving me crazy. I closed my lips over the taut peak, straight through the thin cotton of her blouse and bra. She arched, and another gasp escaped as her fingers speared into my hair.

I needed to feel more of her, so I drew away, swiftly unbuttoning her blouse and pushing it back off her shoulders. She shook her arms slightly, the motion rippling her body and making me acutely aware of the hard, insistent throb of my cock.

I pressed my palm in the center of her chest, feeling the rapid fire of her heartbeat. Her skin was warm. I brushed my thumb over a nipple, and it puckered tighter. Shifting, I flicked the clasp between her breasts, and they tumbled free from her bra.

She let out a ragged whimper when I cupped one plump breast in my palm. Dear God. The sounds she made drove me crazy.

Normally, I was a quiet man when it came to passion. With Ellie, I found myself unable to hold back, murmuring dirty words and teasing comments against her skin.

Dipping my head, I caught her other nipple in my teeth, laving and circling it with my tongue, murmuring against her skin as she cried out. "You feel so fucking good."

When I nipped gently, her hips rocked over my cock, and I let out a growl of satisfaction against her skin.

I was typically measured and orchestrated when it came to sex. Although I didn't doubt my ability to make sure Ellie was satisfied, nothing was calculated.

Ellie's skirt had ridden up around her hips, and I slid my palms along her thighs, my thumbs skimming lightly over the soft sensitive skin at the crease of her hip and thigh. Her hair tickled along my shoulders when she dipped her head, nipping at my neck and sending a hot streak of need through me.

Every touch was electric. The air around us felt heavy, weighted with the desire burgeoning between us. I shifted her back slightly on my lap, cupping my palm over her mound and feeling the damp heat of her through the thin silk.

When I exerted light pressure over her clit with the pad of my thumb, she gasped, "Jacob, I need..." Her words were lost in a groan when I teased with a little more pressure.

"Tell me what you need," I said, watching her in the shadows.

Her hips rocked into my touch, her

breasts brushing against my chest. I suddenly felt as if I had way too many clothes on. The tease of her hard nipples through the cotton was like streaks of fire along my skin.

"More," she gasped when I pressed a little harder.

I deftly hooked a finger over the edge of her panties, pushing them out of the way and groaning when my fingers encountered her drenched folds. She was soaked, slick with arousal.

I stroked through her folds, sinking two fingers into her channel, my cock hardening at the feel of her core rippling around my fingers.

"I need to taste you," I murmured.

I felt more than saw Ellie's eyes widen. Although the darkness surrounding us made everything feel more intense, in some ways, for just a minute, I wished I could see the blush I knew was staining her skin.

Her breath hissed through her teeth as I teased my thumb over her swollen clit. Drawing my fingers away from the heaven of her pussy, I watched her through half-lidded eyes as I lifted my hand to my mouth and sucked the tang of her arousal off my fingers.

She tasted salty and sweet, an elixir to my system. The taste of her galvanized me. The moment my hand fell away, I was catching her lips with mine, sharing the taste with her as I dove into her mouth again, suddenly restless and rushed.

This kiss was almost frantic, and then I broke free, lifting her as I stood. Our clothes came off in a rush. I wasn't usually rough, but I knew I was with her just now, yanking at her skirt and shoving her panties down.

Her hands were as eager as mine, tugging at my buttons and shoving my shirt off my shoulders. She fumbled with my belt, and I nearly tore it apart, pushing my jeans down and kicking them free.

Then, Ellie was against me, her skin silky. I pulled her into my lap again as we tumbled back onto the couch.

Kissing her was like falling into a fire— her mouth warm, her tongue teasing against mine. All of her was soft. I wanted everything all at once, but more than anything, I was driven to be inside of her.

When she straddled me, with her slick folds sliding over my cock, my control almost snapped. Fumbling, I yanked my jeans off the floor where they had fallen by the couch. My wallet conveniently shook loose. In a moment, I had a condom out and was rolling it on, almost losing it when Ellie muttered, "Hurry, please..."

Her hips rose up, and she reached between us. I clung to my control, tightening my grip and savoring the soft give of her flesh under my fingers on her hips. "Wait," I said.

I felt her eyes flick to mine in the darkness. "I want to feel every inch of you," I murmured. I dragged the head of my cock through her folds.

When she cried out, I eased into her, controlling her descent as she sank over me, sheathing me in her core. The walls of her slick channel took me in inch by inch, just as I wanted. The fusion of our joining was so intoxicating, I almost came instantly when she finally got too impatient and sank down abruptly at the end, taking all of me into her.

Her breath was coming in sharp little pants while I could hardly catch mine. I eased my grip on her hips and slid a palm up her spine, levering her forward slightly. Her breasts brushed against my chest, the pointed pressure of her nipples sending hot jolts over my skin. "Kiss me," I said, my request a gruff command.

Ellie didn't hesitate, closing the inches between us, her swollen lips brushing across mine, and her tongue darting out and swiping across my lips. She dove in as she lifted her hips to sink down onto me again.

My usual control dissolved in the heat of the moment. With every rock of her hips, I arched up into her, lost in the madness she had wrought within, my release already threatening to rush through me.

Chapter Nine

ELLIE

Jacob filled me, every long, hard inch of him. The stretch of it was decadent and intoxicating. I felt as if I were spinning, the current tossing me every which way.

Hot, flushed straight through, almost disintegrating in the force of desire pulsing within me, I could barely catch my breath and my pulse was running wild.

This experience with Jacob had almost instantly shown me how out of depth I was with him. Oh, I was no innocent. Yet, I was brutally aware of just how short my last sexual experiences had fallen.

Jacob had ruined me forever.

His touch, so skillful, so strong and sure. He drew me to the edge of release again and again and again. And now, with his words echoing in my mind—*kiss me*—all I could do was comply. One of his hands gripped my hip strongly, controlling the pace as he fucked me into oblivion.

He kissed like no man had ever kissed me —his tongue sweeping in, laying claim to my mouth. His kiss was a mix of rough and hard, soft and gentle. I was moaning into his mouth as his cock filled me and stretched me, over and over and over again. I broke away with a gasp because I needed to breathe. I could feel the heat of his gaze. I was burning up inside.

The fusion of our bodies was slick and wet and tight. Pressure gathered inside of me, spinning and spinning, until he reached between us. With nothing more than a brush of his thumb over my clit, pleasure burst through me, unraveling with such force I nearly blacked out. My release was so intense it almost hurt.

"That's it," he murmured. "Give me just a little more."

He pressed the pad of his thumb against me, and another burst of pleasure scattered through me. I finally felt him let go too, his cock pulsing inside of me.

I collapsed against him, limp in his arms.

In that quiet, dark room, we were wrecked, spent from the intensity that passed between us. I lay collapsed against him, my breath gradually slowing along with the thud of his heartbeat against my ear.

Aside from how absolutely decadent that felt, I was rather stunned. Jacob read my body and responses in a way no man ever had.

I had no sense of time. With the current situation with the blackout, I felt even more disoriented than I usually would. Not that there was anything *usual* about this.

After a few moments, with nothing but the sound of our breathing in the quiet room, I slowly lifted my head from where it had fallen. I felt more than saw Jacob open his eyes from where his head was resting on the couch. He brushed my tangled hair away from my forehead.

The gesture felt strangely intimate and made my heart lurch. Part of me thought I should feel uncomfortable. Yet, I didn't. As out of place and as out of my own element as this could be, I somehow felt completely comfortable with Jacob. The desire between us was so raw and so pure, my defenses fell away.

"Well," I began, having no idea what else

to say.

I saw the hint of his smile in the shadows and felt his low chuckle rumble through his body. "'Well' isn't quite the word for that. Amazing is more like it."

I blushed. I couldn't help it. Not that it mattered because he couldn't see it. A little thrill spun through me, a little hum of joy at his words. I was well over Wayne, but the dents he put in my self-confidence, especially around sex, were still there.

I smiled and leaned forward to press a kiss to Jacob's lips. He slid his hand up my back, cupping my nape and turning it into more than a kiss. I swear, I could've gone another round right then.

He pulled back, his head falling against the couch. "Ellie McNamara. You've ruined me," he said, the gruff sound of his voice striking at my core, playing my body like it was an instrument.

"Somehow, I doubt that," I finally managed in reply.

In the darkness, I couldn't see his expression well, but I sensed a flicker of surprise followed by resolve. "Don't," he said flatly.

Jacob shifted, lifting me in his arms as he slid out of me.

"Where are you going?" I asked as he

deftly adjusted me with one hand hooked under my knees and the other cupping my bottom.

"We might not have any lights, but we have hot water," he replied.

"We do?"

"Water doesn't require power. Because this building is gigantic, I happen to know they've got a huge supply. I'm sure we can get a day or two of showers out of it if necessary, although I'm also fairly sure we'll have power before then."

We showered in the darkness where he kissed me senseless against the tile wall. His fingers skillfully brought me back to another climax in a matter of minutes once he started to soap my body.

I didn't know what I expected, but it wasn't this attentiveness from him. After he tugged me into the bedroom, he checked his phone, and we still had no cell reception. We powered off both of our phones, hoping to conserve the batteries for tomorrow.

That's how I came to fall asleep in Jacob's arms.

I would've thought my mind would keep me awake. But with Jacob's warm, strong arms wrapped around me, I fell into a deep, dreamless sleep.

Chapter Ten

ELLIE

The silvery light of dawn filtered through the sheer window shades on the back wall of the bedroom. I came awake to feel Jacob's hands mapping my body, my nipples tightening, and slick heat building between my thighs. A soft whimper escaped when he lazily cupped one of my breasts, brushing his thumb across the hard peak.

The sound from me appeared to be something he'd been waiting for. He shifted, deftly rolling me over. Then, his lips were tracing their way across my body—the graze of his teeth on a nipple, a swirl of his tongue on the other, a hot, damp kiss on my belly, and his hands gliding up my thighs and pushing my knees apart.

Everything felt as if it were in slow motion—a languid, sensual web of desire spinning around me. Jacob's lips, teeth, tongue, and hands intoxicated me with every touch. He trailed his fingers through my folds as I felt his shoulders press between my thighs, pushing my knees further apart as he murmured soft, dirty words.

"Open for me. Just a little more. I want to taste you because I know how fucking good you taste."

Then, he was looking up at me, his fingers sinking into my channel. I cried out, the pleasure sharp as it rippled through me. He teased me, exploring every inch of me with his tongue. All the while, his fingers fucked me slowly, pushing a little deeper each time as my channel throbbed around him. He brought me to the edge again and again until I was pleading for relief.

He finally gave it to me, sucking my clit. The pleasure hit me like a shock wave, so fierce I went limp in the aftermath, my body shaking from the intensity of my climax.

He rose up over me, and I heard the telltale tear of foil, and then the slow slide of him inside of me, the delicious stretch. His body felt so good against me—hard and strong as he sank into me again and again. I felt my next climax coming in a rush as he pressed over my clit with a deep thrust. My name came in a rough shout as he went rigid before his release whipped through his body.

The moment he fell against me, he rolled us over, so I was laying on top of him.

I rose up on an elbow, looking at him in the wispy light. Jacob opened his eyes, the rich green almost startling in its brightness.

We stared at each other, the moment quiet. With everything occurring last night in the darkness, it was strange to be able to see him a little more clearly now.

His gaze was contemplative. "Good morning, Ellie," he finally said, a slight smile curling the corners of his mouth.

I felt my own smile in return. "Good morning."

His fingers sifted through the ends of my hair where it fell halfway down my back, the touch soothing. After a moment, he said, "I wonder if we have power yet."

He reached over with his free hand to test the lamp sitting on a table beside the bed. The switch clicked, the sound loud in the quiet room.

"This is weird," I said.

Last night, after the initial anxiety, I had entirely lost myself in Jacob, quite effectively blocking out any fears about the blackout. Now, even though he had once again made me forget everything else in the world, reality intruded, and it was rather unsettling.

Jacob's hand slid out of my hair and down my back in a smooth stroke. "Don't worry just yet. It hasn't even been twenty-four hours. Let's shower and scrounge up something to eat here. I'll consider whether we should sit tight, or if I should venture out."

"Just you?"

His eyes met mine, his gaze somber. "You can come with me," he finally said. "It's just, I don't know what's going on."

"I'd rather stay with you, whether you go somewhere, or stay here."

He leaned up, pressing his lips firmly to mine. "Then, whatever we do, we do together."

At that, I rose up, and we untangled ourselves. We kept our shower brief. Afterward, we each checked our phones, just long enough to confirm there was still no cell reception. With no power, all the Wi-Fi was out, so there was no way for us to know what was going on outside where we were, and if this blackout extended beyond downtown Las Vegas.

The windows on this ground floor suite

looked out into an inner courtyard of the hotel. As such, we weren't able to see out into
the main streets, although Jacob assured me
we could do so from the office section of
where we were.

He stepped out to check, and I could tell
he wanted to dissuade me from following,
but I was determined. I glanced out into the
street to find not much of anything. It was
only six a.m., so I didn't expect much. There
were a few cars moving, and some people out
and about. The tone was more subdued.
Clearly, during the night, many had returned
to where they were staying.

In the early morning light, Las Vegas
seemed strange with all the neon signs off.
You didn't think much about the rumble of
power running in the background until it was
gone.

"I'll take it as a win that people seem
mostly calm," Jacob murmured as he closed
the shade to the window. "Let's see what we
can rustle up for food and coffee."

His palm glided down my back, coming
to rest at the dip of my waist and coaxing me
into the suite in the back of the offices. He
didn't say it aloud, but I could tell he was
concerned about anyone noticing our presence in here.

"What are you worried about?' I asked, once we were in the back again, and he had bolted the door behind us.

"People do crazy things when they're not sure what's happening. Obviously, Darren knows we're here, so I'm not worried about that. But I *am* worried about anyone else thinking we might have something they want."

With the sun rising and its rays angling through the windows, I was able to see the space beyond shadows. It was furnished simply, but luxuriously. The couch was a soft dove gray with side chairs to match. The small kitchen area had an oval shaped island and modern stainless-steel appliances.

There wasn't much food to be found, as Darren had warned us, but there was instant oatmeal, some granola bars, and coffee.

"How are we going to make coffee?" I asked.

"Propane stove," Jacob replied with a wink. "It'll work without power."

He boiled water and poured the coffee grounds in the bottom of the saucepan, explaining to me that the grounds would settle. In a few minutes, we enjoyed our instant oatmeal and granola bars with coffee.

The quiet simplicity of the morning

struck me. Las Vegas had literally felt like a humming, pulsating center of power prior to the blackout. This morning, it felt subdued.

My thoughts kept wandering toward last night with Jacob. Each time, I dashed away from them mentally. I wanted him fiercely. Still.

Yet, I wanted to keep last night encapsulated. Jacob was who he was, and there was no way our lives could match. Not to mention, it was crazy for me to even think he wanted anything more than sex from me. I mean, good grief, he was a billionaire. Not exactly the kind of man who would be interested in someone like me. Not that I was wont to care about money, but I was quite practical.

I was an artist. I made my living and sometimes barely scraped by with whatever project I was working on at the time. I'd been lucky enough to stumble into a few profitable setups with galleries in Bellingham and Seattle. My fabric arts and pottery were my most profitable and seemed to pay the bills, no matter what. My life was a far cry from Jacob's. Although my brother was friends with him, that was because Aidan worked in security and ran one of the premier companies in Seattle. But Aidan wasn't like Jacob either. Then, to be fair, I didn't know a whole lot about Jacob beyond last night.

I sipped my coffee after I finished my oatmeal and looked over at him. "So, what now?"

Chapter Eleven

JACOB

"So, what now?" Ellie's question echoed in my mind.

I considered our options. We could sit tight, although the idea of sitting in one place when we didn't know what the hell was going on chafed at me. The other option was to head out and assess the status. Darren and his family lived a good mile away. If we were to go anywhere, that would be the place.

If I were only considering myself, I would definitely leave. Ellie had made it clear she was not interested in waiting here if I left. With the uncertainty of the situation, I could leave and end up having difficulty reaching her again.

I wasn't much of an alarmist. Yet, I'd seen

more than enough and read more than enough dystopia stories to have plenty of grist for my imagination to run wild. Not to mention my expertise with security. I knew quite well there were plenty of issues for us to worry about.

So far, the only concern was we had no power. As for my focus, let's just say it wasn't up to par.

Last night with Ellie had blown the doors off my heart. Just being near her was its own challenge. My cock appeared to have an opinion about everything—all but yelling that I couldn't let Ellie out of my sight.

"Jacob?" she prompted.

I sipped my coffee, which came out pretty damn good, all things considered. "Either we wait, or we go investigate," I finally said.

"Investigate what?"

"The situation, I suppose. Darren, who you met last night, lives about a mile away. With security his specialty, he's got every potential backup you could imagine at his home. We can walk, and along the way, we might hear some updates."

Ellie stared at me, her teeth denting her bottom lip, the sight of it reminding me of how her lips felt under mine. A jolt of need hit me.

Fuck me. I needed to get a handle on my body around her.

Her hazel eyes met mine, that swirl of green, gold, and nutmeg almost hypnotizing. She let out a soft sigh, lifting a hand and twirling a lock of her glossy black hair around her finger.

"I'm guessing if it weren't for me, you would've already left."

After a beat, I nodded. "But you *are* here, so we stick together," I said simply.

I was rather stunned at the fierce protectiveness I felt toward her. Considering she was Aidan's sister, I would've felt a sense of responsibility to ensure that she was okay, no matter what. But this was different.

One word repeated on a loop in my mind. *Mine. Mine. Mine.*

Whether she could sense my internal reaction or not, a pink flush crested on her cheeks, and I wanted to kiss her all over. As intense as last night and this morning had been, everything had been in shades of darkness. I couldn't fucking wait to have her when I could see everything so clearly.

She started to open her mouth, and I anticipated her question before she spoke. I shook my head sharply. "Don't even ask. I'm not going anywhere without you."

Her lips twitched at the corners with a smile. "Okay. Well then, let's just do what you would whether or not I was here."

"All right, let's go to Darren's."

We were ready to go within a few minutes. I debated whether to leave my laptop here or not, eventually settling on leaving it here. So far, things seemed quiet, so I hedged my bets the power would be restored and we'd stop back by here later. When we got to the door, before we stepped out of the office part of the suite, I paused and glanced back at Ellie.

She looked fresh-faced and far too wholesome. Not in the sense of experience, but more that life hadn't been too cold to her just yet. Somehow, she still wasn't that cynical, not like me.

Her wholesomeness was what made the way I felt about her even more startling. She was mistaken if she thought last night would be our only night. Not if I had my way.

"Stick close to me. Things are quiet right now, but it's early. If we don't get some sort of answer about why there's no power and no cell reception soon, I imagine anxiety might start to peak," I said.

Ellie nodded. "I'm stuck to you like glue," she said, so earnestly I couldn't help but smile. Before I realized what I was doing, I bent low, sliding my hand into her hair to cup her nape and catch her lips in a kiss.

The moment our lips met, it was as if electricity sizzled in the air between us, zinging hot through me and tightening my body with need. Again.

Rattled by the power of my reaction to her, I drew back. "Let's go."

With her hand held firmly in mine, we left. I had left the laptop in a small safe. Worst case scenario, the offices got ransacked. Best case scenario, the power came back on and we would be back at the penthouse within a few hours.

I led Ellie along a winding route out of this building, purposefully exiting on the far side from where we'd stayed. Once we stepped out onto the street, I was relieved to find the streets mostly quiet, with only a few people walking. In Las Vegas, that was rather typical. Night and day were almost reversed here as far as activity.

That said, the streets were not empty. I paused beside an elderly gentleman wearing the uniform for the hotel, where he stood in front of the entrance. "Any updates?" I asked.

He glanced to me, his gaze inscrutable until he appeared to recognize who I was. There were many downsides to my unexpected success with my business. Perhaps the biggest one was I never knew when complete strangers would recognize me. Further, I didn't know what that would mean to them.

The man glanced from me to Ellie and back again before shrugging and shaking his head. "Nothing. I'm concerned if we don't get the power back soon, people are going to start getting stressed out."

"Exactly my concern. We'll be back this way later," I added, turning and heading in the direction of Darren's place.

Ellie was quiet as we walked, but I could practically feel the questions tumbling in her mind. She finally spoke. "When do you think something will come on?"

"No idea. We're going to pass a police station on the way to Darren's. I'm guessing if anyone's got their generators up and running, they will. It won't surprise me if Darren does either."

Ellie nodded, giving my hand a squeeze. I kept telling myself as we walked that perhaps my response to her was heightened by the uncertainty of events around us. Every time I told myself that, I remembered the heated joining of our bodies.

Ellie's head came just above my shoulders, yet her stride was long and she had no trouble keeping up with me. The police station was where I had recalled, but there was a line outside despite the early hour. I immediately angled to the opposite side of the street. Glancing to Ellie, I said, "No need to stop. I can hear their generators, and Darren's probably already been down there anyway."

I tried to ignore the tension building inside, but it was difficult. I didn't like uncertainty. In fact, my entire career, regardless of my reasons for stumbling into it, was built to create contingencies to avoid uncertainty.

I hoped like hell when we got to Darren's, his backup power was working. If I were back in Seattle, I would've already had power to my computer. We turned onto the street where Darren's home was. Although he lived in downtown Las Vegas, he was in a small gated and highly secure community, set back off one of the main thoroughfares.

As I saw the entrance come into sight, I contemplated how to alert him we were here. Blessedly, we didn't have to. He approached from across the street, waving to us with a dog at his side and the leash looped in his hand.

We paused to wait. "Hey there, man," I said as soon as he reached us.

Darren grinned. "Morning. Figured you might head this way. Just out walking one of my daughter's dogs from the shelter where she volunteers. When the power went out last night, she brought this guy home."

A smile stretched across Ellie's face, her features softening as she looked down at the dog. The dog in question was a shaggy brown mutt, as best I could guess.

"Oh, hi." The joy was evident in her tone as she stroked her hand along the dog's back. "What's the dog's name?" she asked, glancing up to Darren.

"Chocolate. Nice to see you when it's not dark," he offered with a wink.

"You too. Did they find places for all the dogs?" she asked.

"As far as I know. My daughter volunteers there to walk the dogs. We took two. The other one is a tiny little thing, and she can barely walk in a circle in the yard. Chocolate and I decided to take a longer route," Darren explained.

Chocolate appeared as enamored with

Ellie as I was, rubbing his head on her knees and tail wagging madly at her side.

"Any luck getting power here?" I asked.

"Of course. Our generator's working fine."

Ellie straightened, and I noticed the tightness in her features ease. I hated to think she was worried and was taken aback by just how much it mattered to me that she didn't worry. At all. I wanted to wall her off from anything.

"Anyway, follow me," Darren said. He glanced to Ellie. "Want to be in charge of Chocolate?"

Ellie's answering smile was like a ray of sunshine, casting light straight into my cynical heart. My sister's story was well-known. Not because I chose to make it so, but because people were nosy as fucking hell. After my sister didn't accept a second date with a wealthy doctor, she ended up dying in a car accident. So did he. In the very same accident. To this day, no one could prove he intended to kill her, but I knew he had. I had seen the messages he sent her.

They had met over a dating app. She did all the right things to keep herself safe on their first date. She met him in a busy, public place and took a cab to get there. He shouldn't have been able to find out where she lived, but he did. So, I developed another app that created layers of protection around online communications and ways to protect yourself. I wasn't the most trusting guy after what happened to my sister.

Ellie was like a bracing breath of fresh air. Even though she had lost both of her parents, and even though she had an ex who cheated on her with a friend, she was still hopeful and still open.

Darren handed her the leash. "You and my daughter can bond over your shared love of all things dogs."

With a key, he led us through the back gate into the complex. All the while, Ellie murmured to Chocolate and occasionally replied to Darren and I, adding as we approached his front door, "I foster rescues in Seattle. My last dog passed away about six months ago, so I've been trying to decide when I'll get another one."

Darren grinned. "Well, be prepared for my daughter to try to sweet talk you into keeping Chocolate." He paused at a corner. "So, you live in Seattle, like Aidan?"

Ellie nodded. "Sure do." She paused, concern flashing in her eyes. "I'm sure he'll be worried about the blackout."

"Oh, I've already talked to Aidan. Told him I saw you last night," Darren commented as he led us along a winding walkway.

"You did?" Ellie asked, her gaze swinging to Darren. "Does he have any idea what's going on?"

Chapter Twelve

ELLIE

Darren turned down their driveway, answering me as he fit the key in the door. "Little bit, all we know is what happened. We don't know the source."

"What happened?" Jacob asked. "Some kind of electrical grid shut down is my guess."

Darren nodded as he closed the door behind us, just as a tiny, ancient-looking Chihuahua walked gingerly into the entryway from an archway off to the side.

Chocolate gave a little tug on the leash, but I held firm and looked up to Darren. "Is he okay to be loose now?"

"Oh yes, he's friendly as can be and surprisingly gentle."

Unclipping the leash, I watched as

Chocolate trotted over to the tiny Chihuahua, who froze in place while Chocolate gently nudged her with his nose.

I wanted to take them both home. Clearly, they had a good place to stay for the time being, and somehow, seeing the dogs had settled me inside. Animals were my passion. I had fostered them for years and was constantly struggling with the urge to adopt every one of them.

Although I was watching the dogs, I glanced over when Darren responded to another question from Jacob. "Yep. The electrical grid and cell towers shut down throughout Las Vegas, but it was only on the Strip where generators were sabotaged."

"How the hell did you get through to Aidan?" Jacob asked.

"With the generator, our Wi-Fi works just fine."

Jacob chuckled. "Of course, wasn't thinking."

A woman stepped out into the hallway. She was stunning, with rich nutmeg hair and bright blue eyes. She was dressed casually, in sweatpants and a T-shirt, and smiled when she saw Jacob. "Jacob! Darren figured you would find us this morning. Come on back. I'm making breakfast."

"We had coffee and oatmeal on your own propane stove in that apartment, but a real meal would be great," Jacob replied.

The woman approached me, holding her hand out. "Hello, I'm Sarah," she said with a warm smile, shaking my hand.

"I'm Ellie. Thank goodness I ran into Jacob last night. I don't know what I would have done if I hadn't."

Sarah nodded. "I'm glad you found him too. Come on back, you can meet our daughter, Dee."

We followed her through the archway with Darren gesturing for us to walk ahead of him. We passed through what appeared to be a sitting room and down a short hallway that led to a kitchen. Windows looked out over the backyard and a teenage girl with her mother's coloring sat at the counter on a stool, her feet swinging.

"Chocolate!" she exclaimed as she slid off the stool and hurried over to greet the dog. The Chihuahua stopped beside me as Chocolate scurried over to meet the girl. I paused to kneel down beside her. Her face was all gray and her once black hair was mostly silver now. She sniffed my hand and nuzzled my knuckles when I rubbed them under her chin.

"What's your name?" I asked the little dog conversationally.

"Janice," the daughter replied. After greeting Chocolate, she walked across the kitchen to scoop Janice up in her arms. The small dog immediately burrowed into her chest, letting out a contented sigh.

Sarah glanced from me to her daughter with a smile. "This is Ellie, Jacob's friend." Pausing, she looked to me. "And this is Dee."

Dee smiled. "Nice to meet you. You like dogs?"

"Most definitely. I foster them for a rescue program in Seattle."

"Do you have your own?"

I felt Jacob's eyes on me as Sarah rounded an island in the kitchen, asking Darren something.

"Not right now. I love fostering, although the hardest part is I want to keep them all. But if I did that, then I wouldn't be able to keep doing it," I said with a shrug, reaching out to rub my knuckles under Janice's chin again. She let out another contented sigh and closed her eyes.

Dee smiled down at her. "We're going to keep Janice, but we can't keep them all either." She turned, carrying Janice over to a dog bed sitting on the windowsill in a patch of sun. It was clearly there for this reason. Dee carefully set Janice down in the bed. She opened her eyes long enough to turn in a circle and settled into the sunshine. It was a perfect napping spot.

Over the next hour or so, Sarah cooked everyone breakfast, making scrambled eggs with bacon and hash browns. The meal, simple though it was, felt quite decadent given that most of the city was without power.

Darren pulled up his laptop and contacted Aidan through a secured messaging system. I let Aidan know I was fine and asked him if he knew anything. All he could tell me was they suspected a hack of the grid, and he was worried. He assured me if this didn't resolve soon, we could drive out of Las Vegas and fly out another way.

It was strange because while Las Vegas was humming, it felt as if you were in the center of a unique universe that snapped and crackled with energy and electricity. With the heartbeat of Vegas without power, it felt much quieter.

After breakfast, I found myself sitting on the couch with Jacob's arm curled around my shoulders. The weight of it was comforting and strong. His presence was quiet and steady, and such a turn on, I didn't know what to do with myself.

In a way, I had taken this trip to Las Vegas almost out of spite. I had the plane ticket, and it was nonrefundable. I should have known Wayne would decide to take Cheryl. Despite my efforts not to dwell on him and Cheryl, it was impossible not to know they were still together. I felt petty for hoping he would screw Cheryl over just the way he screwed me over.

I was luckier than I could've imagined having Jacob stumble across us in the casino. If that hadn't happened, my mortification would've run even deeper. I would've moved out of the room that had been reserved on Wayne's credit card, making the whole situation sting even more.

Somehow none of that seemed to matter anymore. My mind flashed to last night—the shadowy darkness, the feel of Jacob filling me, the spinning intensity of my climax rushing over me and leaving me boneless and sated. Then, this morning in the thin light of dawn, his hands and fingers once again sending me flying.

Of all the things I had expected from this trip, last night was definitely *not* one of them —the hottest night of my life in the arms of an incredibly sexy and inscrutable billionaire. Just thinking about it made me flush straight through.

It was clear Sarah and Darren were treating us as a couple. Jacob interacted with me comfortably, his affection light and easy. I didn't know how to read it, but I didn't know him well enough to interpret much of anything.

My mind kept turning over last night and this morning. I was rather shocked at how comfortable I felt with him. While the attraction was undeniable, when I decided to snatch a hold of it and see it through, I had expected to feel a sense of nervousness.

Yet, with Jacob, the sheer force of need roaring through my body overtook everything. There was something raw and honest between us. I had no idea what to think of it and resolved not to read too much into it. Last night was *one* night—out of time and place, and completely removed from my regular life. The power would come back on, and I would fly home soon.

Chapter Thirteen

JACOB

Later that morning, the power came back on. Ellie and I remained at Darren's for the rest of the day if only to avoid the rush of activity returning to the Strip. Their home was large and comfortable. Darren and I fiddled around, attempting to chase down possibilities that caused the power outage with Aidan and a few of our respective security contacts scattered across the country. Everyone had hypotheses, but in the end, no one knew who had caused the complete power outage and knocked out the cell communications on the Strip in Las Vegas.

Ellie had spent most of the day chatting with Sarah and Dee. She clearly had a soft spot for the dogs. Chocolate curled up on the couch with her in the afternoon while she and Dee played cards.

As the day wore on, I realized I could get used to this with her. Aidan had asked me to look out for Ellie when we were messaging back and forth. My conscience snapped at me. I imagined he didn't include me fucking her brains out twice in a twelve-hour span as part of "looking out for her."

My jaded, cynical mind was getting some serious pushback from my heart, which certainly had an opinion about all kinds of things. Well, not all kinds of things. Just Ellie. My heart kept telling me she was worth it. That just because my sister died didn't mean I needed to be alone for the rest of my life. That I could use Ellie's unwavering hopefulness in life. Not to mention my raging need for her.

More than anything, I knew what I felt with her last night and again this morning was more rare than a fucking unicorn. If there was such a thing as unicorn sex, I had it last night with Ellie.

Unicorn sex turned out to be the hottest sex of my life. If today hadn't had its unique circumstances, I was quite certain I would still be tangled up skin-to-skin with her. I honestly didn't know if I could get enough of her. Ever.

A small part of me was disappointed when the power came back on. Although my rational, reasonable brain definitely wanted things back to normal, there was a tiny corner of my mind that had enjoyed the quiet last night. Without it, I doubted if I would have allowed myself the opportunity to tumble into my night with Ellie.

Later in the afternoon, Ellie and I prepared to return back to the penthouse with a plan to stop by Darren's offices to fetch my laptop. Ellie was sitting on the couch with Chocolate half on her lap as she idly stroked his ears, smiling at something Dee said.

Looking at her, my heart clenched, the sensation unfamiliar. She was too good for me, or that's what I needed to keep telling myself. Darren paused at my side where I was leaning in the archway, looking at Ellie.

"You got it bad," he said with a low laugh.

I tore my gaze from Ellie to look at him. "Excuse me?"

Darren's lips quirked with a smile. "You're usually cool, calm, never paying attention to the women clamoring for your attention. I don't really know what's up with you and Ellie, but don't even try to tell me you don't have a thing for her."

I took a deep breath and let it out with a sigh, abruptly deciding I didn't care to lie. "Okay, I won't then. Aidan would fucking kick my ass."

Darren glanced to Ellie, his gaze considering. Meanwhile, she lifted a hand, tucking a lock of her glossy hair behind her ear. I suddenly remembered the soft scent of her along the downy skin of her neck. I vividly recalled the feel of her skin prickling under my lips.

Darren's gaze flicked back to me. "Maybe he will. But the way you look at her, it's more than just some kind of casual fling. There's nothing wrong with settling down, you know?"

My eyes widened, unable to hide my shock. "Look, I might like her, but I think you're getting ahead of yourself."

Darren's smile was knowing. He held my gaze as Sarah called his name. "I don't think so, man."

———

The sound of ice clinking in a glass reached me. A few hours ago, we had returned to our hotel suite. It said something that I was now thinking of it as *ours*.

Ellie had announced she wanted a long shower to ground her once we got here. Then, she had a call with Aidan.

Meanwhile, I had hopped onto my various networks, unable to resist poking around in the nether regions of the online world to see if I could chase down the source of the power outage. Curiosity was my longtime companion.

At the sound of the ice settling, I glanced up from where I was sitting on the couch, my eyes landing on Ellie. She was so damn beautiful she took my breath away. She wore another one of those stretchy skirts that hugged her hips and flared out around her knees. Her hair was down, the glossy fall masking her face from my view as she looked down and poured what I presumed to be whiskey into the glass tumbler.

I instantly lost interest in what I was doing and found myself standing and striding across the room. I reached her just as she began to turn. She must not have heard me approaching because her mouth dropped open, her breath coming out in a small gasp. My cock had started to swell the moment I noticed her. Now, it ached. For her.

"Hey," I said softly, resting my hands on either side of her hips and curling my fingers around the curved edge of the bar.

The scent of her wound around me like smoke, catching me, the flames threatening to engulf us both. I felt a fine tremor run through her, and she lifted the tumbler to sip her whiskey. Her lips glistened as she lowered the glass, her tongue darting out and sliding across her plump bottom lip.

Lust struck me so hard it was like a bolt of lightning. The air around us hummed to life. Ellie's kaleidoscope eyes darkened as she stared at me. "Hey," she replied belatedly, her voice raspy and catching at my heart.

My need for her was intoxicating. Yet somehow, the emotions she stirred up were even more so. I felt off-balance. The ground under my feet, usually firm and predictably stable, was shaking.

Ellie was my only anchor. I uncurled one hand from the bar, reaching between us to take the whiskey from her and sip the cool liquor. It was so quiet in the room, I could've heard a spider lift one of its legs and set it on the floor. The subtle burn of the whiskey seemed fitting. Being near Ellie was like playing with fire.

I sucked one of the small ice cubes into

my mouth and set the tumbler down on the bar behind us, sliding it back out of the way. Then, I dipped my head, savoring her slight gasp.

Still holding the ice under my tongue, I pressed my cool lips against her. A hum of satisfaction came from my throat when she arched into me. Goose bumps rose on her skin under my lips as I made my way down, tracing over her collarbone before dipping into the valley between her breasts.

Conveniently, the blouse she wore this evening had a deep V. The sheer fabric did little to disguise the hard peaks of her nipples pressing against it. The ice was melting, and I let it slip out where it slid down between her breasts. Ellie sucked in a breath, her hand curling over the collar of my T-shirt.

Fuck me. I'd never paid much attention at all to the sounds women made. With Ellie, each sound was a light lash of a whip, driving my desire to churn faster and faster inside of me.

"Jacob," she whispered, the sound skating over my skin.

I leaned forward, catching that last sliver of ice with my tongue and dragging it out as it melted against her skin. Somewhere along the way, I had lifted a hand to cup one of her breasts, and I felt her nipple pebble more tightly under my thumb.

I was nearly out of my mind with need for her, but I clung to my control. Lifting my head, I met her gaze. Her pupils were dilated, her eyes wide, and her skin flushed. "Yes?"

"I thought last night was just a one-time thing," she said, her voice just barely above a whisper.

She had every right to point out that little detail. I didn't remember if I had said it would be just once. But then, even if I had, I couldn't have anticipated how it would affect me. Instead of slaking my need for her, the opposite had occurred.

I held her gaze, searching her eyes. Although I saw vulnerability and uncertainty flickering in the depths, I also saw that raw, pure need reflected back at me, that search for connection that had taken us both by surprise.

I didn't know what I wanted, not beyond this moment. I sensed Ellie was wandering in the same mix of confusion and need. I preferred not to think about the future. Once you see someone's future snuffed out, as I had with my sister, it cuts the cord you cling to. You learn to try to make the best of the moment because that's all there really is when the rest falls away.

I didn't mean that in a spiritual way, more in a practical, brutally realistic way.

Just now, here in this burning hot, electric moment, all I wanted was Ellie. I didn't want to contemplate anything else. Or perhaps I did.

"What do you want tonight?" I asked, my voice taut with the lust that gripped me.

I could feel the heat of her skin through the thin silk of her blouse and the soft, rapid beat of her heart. Her pulse fluttered wildly along her neck, a flush staining her skin everywhere and making me want to tear her clothes off and see all of her bare.

As intoxicating as last night had been in the darkness, I desperately wanted to see her fly apart with my eyes wide open and her in bright color.

"*You*," she said her word coming out forcefully.

With that, she tightened her grip on the collar of my shirt, tugging me to her. The moment her lips met mine, it was as if a match was thrown into the banked embers between us. Flames caught and licked around us.

Although there was that wholesome sultriness to Ellie, she wasn't innocent, and she was so damn responsive. Everything she did was like a straight shot into the vein of my need.

Her hand uncurled from my collar, and she flexed against me, sliding it up to cup the nape of my neck and kiss me as if her life depended on it. I was so ready, riding the edge of my control in a way I never had before.

I tugged at her blouse, careless with the buttons, barely registering the sound of one pinging against the floor somewhere. As soon as her blouse fell open, I tore my lips from hers and dipped my head, sucking at her nipple right through the silk of her bra. I growled, a surge of satisfaction rushing through me when she cried out and arched forward, offering up her fucking perfect breasts for the taking.

She yanked at my shirt, impatient enough to swear when I stayed busy teasing her nipples and flicking open the clasp between her breasts, drawing back slightly just so I could see them. They tumbled loose, round and plump, the skin flushed pink like I knew she would be once I got her naked.

"Get this off," she murmured, shoving her hands up under my shirt, the feel of her palms sliding against my skin sending a shot of blood straight to my groin.

Stepping back, I reached behind my neck and yanked my shirt off, tossing it to the floor. Ellie's hands traveled over my chest, her lips stringing kisses in the wake of her touch. Just when I meant to take control, she ripped it right out of my hands. She made quick work of the buttons on my fly, flicking them open and sliding her hand down into my briefs.

The feel of her lightly stroking my cock nearly pushed me beyond the edge. "Ellie," I growled, meaning to say something, anything, to get my bearings again.

She murmured something just as her lips dusted more kisses along my abs, and she pushed my briefs down, freeing my cock. Before I could catch my breath, I felt the warmth of her lips closing around the tip of my cock, the vibration of her humming nearly unleashing my release instantly.

My hand tangled in her hair as I held on. With a subtle push, she rotated us so my hips were pressed against the bar, and she shimmied to her knees. When I glanced down to see her blouse falling open and her pretty pink nipples, she looked up with a sly smile. Her tongue darted out to swipe a drop of precum rolling off the tip of my cock, and my hand tightened in her hair.

Her tongue swirled around the head, and I couldn't look away. She was so fucking hot and sexy. I'd had plenty of women suck me off. But no one did it like Ellie. She nearly made my knees buckle when she dragged her tongue along the underside of my cock, her fist lightly gripping at the base right before she sucked me deeply into the warm suction of her mouth.

I barely recognized the rough groan coming from me. I felt as if I were hanging on for dear life, one hand curled over the bar and the other in her hair. She worked me with her mouth, her tongue swirling as she sucked me in again before drawing back, her fist sliding up and down along the slick moisture she left behind.

She teased me, taking me to the edge again and again. I meant to tell her I didn't want to come inside her mouth, that I didn't want to let go until I was buried as deeply inside of her as I could get.

But she gave me no choice. At the sight of her lips, swollen and glistening as she swirled her tongue around the head of my cock again before she drew me in and sucked just hard enough to pull my orgasm from me, whether I wanted it or not. My balls tightened, and heat twisted at the base of my spine, lightning jolting through me as I poured my release into her mouth.

She took every drop before pulling back slowly, her tongue swirling around her lips. So damn sexy. I was hard again before she even fully straightened.

Chapter Fourteen

ELLIE

I rose to my feet, feeling the heat of Jacob's gaze on me. Dear God. The man was obscenely handsome. He stood there, his jeans half-open, and his cock hardening again right before my eyes. His hand fell from my hair when I straightened.

His chest was a glorious wall of muscle, the soft lighting casting shadows across his bronzed skin. Everything between us felt like hot lava. I felt as if I were diving into it, yet it didn't burn. The sensation held me in its fire, burning everything else in my awareness to ashes.

Jacob's eyes took on a gleam, the wicked look sending my belly into a flip and tingles spinning through my veins. I felt so alive when I was with him, my nerves sparking everywhere.

My panties were soaked, and I shifted my thighs to relieve the ache building there. I sensed when he noticed, and his lips kicked up slightly at one corner. He pushed away from the bar, closing the few inches between us, and lifted his hands to slide my blouse and bra off my shoulders. I barely heard the fabric rumple to the floor. His hands traced down my sides into the dip of my waist, his subtle touch eliciting a whimper.

This intensity with him came so easily. When I was in the midst of it, everything felt like a slow, sensual dance, and as if we were the only two people in the world.

When his palms reached my hips, he hooked his thumbs over the stretchy waist-band, dragging my fitted skirt down over my hips. It fell around my ankles, and I lifted one foot at a time, kicking off my shoes and sending the skirt spinning on the floor to the side.

I stood bare before him, save my panties. As intense as last night had been, and again this morning, everything had occurred in darkness. This morning had been the thin, silvery light of dawn, that in-between time that felt not quite real.

This moment, here tonight, with everything back in order, I felt suddenly exposed as I stood before him.

"Ellie, you're so beautiful," he murmured.

I felt hot all over, anxious for him to get closer. I desperately *needed* to lose myself in him, in *us*. He stepped closer and lifted me into his arms. He spun us around, sliding my hips onto the cool wood of the bar.

Straightening, he watched me as he teased his fingers over the damp silk between my thighs. Shoving it out of the way, he dragged his fingers through my folds, and I let out a gasp, my hips bucking into his touch.

"Jacob, please," I heard myself saying, my tone pleading. I was *that* frantic, *that* needy. It wasn't purely physical, although my physical need was bordering on out of control. It was more than that. I needed the connection because that was the only thing that could anchor me in this wild storm of sensation running amok in my body.

Jacob curled his hands on my hips and slid them to the edge of the bar, lifting me easily as he yanked my panties off. Before I realized what he was doing, he had reached behind me. The sound of clinking came as he fished out a piece of ice. Watching me, he drew back and teased it over my hot core, the icy cold such a stark contrast I cried out, my eyes widening.

It melted just as he dipped his head, his teeth grazing along my neck. The feel of his stubble scratching on my skin was a welcome relief, anything to give me something to focus on other than where I needed him most.

"Don't make me wait," I cried out when he caught a nipple in his teeth, sucking it lightly.

"I like it when you're bossy," he murmured against my skin as he nudged a little closer between my knees. I felt him dragging the head of his cock through my folds, sliding over my swollen clit. I was so close. It had never been like this before, where foreplay alone could bring me right up to the edge of release. In fact, orgasms with anyone other than myself were so few and far between, I considered it luck if it happened.

Jacob appeared to be the exception. *He* alone was enough, my own personal aphrodisiac and elixir rolled up in a delicious hard body with teasing fingers and a tongue that seemed to know me in ways I didn't even know myself.

"Look at me," he said gruffly as he pressed into me, the head of his cock breaching my entrance, enough of a tease to make me want more, to crave the stretch.

At his gruff command, I opened my eyes. His dark gaze was waiting, intent on me, a wildness in his eyes which mirrored the way I felt inside.

Then, there was the slow slide, his thick, hard length filling me. By the time he sank to the hilt, my climax was cresting.

"Not yet," he said, his voice harsh and his fingers digging into my hip as he held me still. My channel rippled around him, and I clung to my control.

"I don't know if I can hold back," I gasped.

"Just once," he murmured in reply as he drew his hips back and then surged inside forcefully, his thumb pressing over my clit right as he filled me.

My release hit me hard, snapping like a bolt breaking loose inside and pleasure crashing through me when I cried out. I dimly heard my name in his rough shout.

Jacob's head fell into the dip against my neck, and I felt the shudders of his climax. My breath came in ragged gasps. I was relieved to be sitting on the bar because I doubted I could hold myself up otherwise.

The room was quiet save for the sound of

our rough breathing and the rush of blood pounding in my ears. My pulse gradually slowed, and I felt Jacob lift his head.

I was limp, barely able to lift my head from where it had fallen against his chest. When I opened my eyes, he brushed my tangled hair away from my forehead, smoothing it back.

When our eyes collided, my heart squeezed. Something electric passed between us—invisible, but intense. With the aftershocks of my climax still echoing through my body, thoughts couldn't quite form. I felt as if I were spinning in the eddies of a wave after it broke along the edge of the shore.

"I meant to ask if you wanted to go out to dinner," Jacob said softly, his words a mere rasp.

I sensed he was trying to get his footing, just as I was. For that, I was relieved. I could hardly wrap my brain around how fierce the desire was between us. The moment we touched, it was like a flame catching in dry grass, instantly becoming a conflagration. With my heart still not fully recovered and my body feeling as if glitter was spinning through it, I stared into his eyes and smiled.

"Dinner would be nice," I finally managed to say. His lips quirked, a smile stretching across his face and making my belly do a little flip.

"All right then," he replied, leaning forward and brushing his lips against mine.

What was nothing more than a brief touch, an almost chaste kiss, sent a sizzle of electricity right to my core.

Jacob stepped away, starting to slide out of me, his eyes colliding with mine swiftly. "Oh shit. I forgot to use a condom. Hell, I'm sorry, Ellie. I'm usually thinking more clearly."

He looked quite stunned. I imagined he usually did think. So did I. But when it came to him, my ability to think seemed to go up in smoke.

"It's okay," I replied quickly. "I'm on birth control. And, if you're worried about anything else, don't. I'm clean. After what happen with Wayne last year, I got tested for everything because I didn't know what else he'd been up to," I said, my words coming out in a stumbling rush. "I haven't had sex with anyone since then. Well, except you."

Jacob studied me quietly and then nodded. "I wasn't worried about that. It's a respect thing for me. You seem to make me lose my mind," he said with a short laugh. "I can assure you I'm clean. Because this would be the first time I've *ever* forgotten to use a condom."

I took a deep breath, letting it out slowly. "Well then, I guess if it happens again, we don't need to worry."

Jacob stared at me, his gaze searching. "Oh, it'll happen again. That's a damn guarantee."

I didn't know how to interpret that, or what to say in reply, so I was relieved when he stepped back. His palms skimmed down my thighs as he drew away.

Quickly, he returned, helping me slide off the bar. Not that I needed his help, but somehow it made me feel protected. That wasn't a feeling I had ever craved, yet it felt so good I didn't know what to think.

I took stock, finding myself bare naked, and my clothes scattered like confetti around us. My skirt was in a rumple over near the couch, my blouse and bra were on the floor to one side, my shoes were to the other, and my panties had been flung almost to the wall. Jacob's shirt had fallen beside my skirt. He leaned over, quickly gathering up our things.

Glancing to him, I commented, "Be right back."

We quickly tidied up and got dressed. When we were leaving for dinner, Jacob's hand rested warm just above the curve of my bottom, his touch both reassuring and coaxing at once. I realized as we stepped into the elevator that I would've been perfectly happy to stay in and lose myself in him all over again.

Chapter Fifteen

JACOB

Two days passed. Two days during which I practically worshipped at the altar of Ellie.

After the power came back on, everything largely returned to normal as far as Las Vegas was concerned. The snap and crackle of the city that was always alive and pulsing kicked right back into gear. The conference —the reason I was there—resumed and quickly extended itself for a day. Considering that everything had come to a screeching stop for a day, that made sense.

I managed to go through the motions and seem focused, yet I was in a bit of a fog. Ellie had crashed into my life like an asteroid, blowing it up and shifting everything. The sex was incredible. Beyond incredible. I couldn't get enough.

Meanwhile, I was busy assessing every contingency and trying to figure out how I was going to persuade her she was meant to be mine. When we were together, there was no doubt. Not for me.

Yet, I sensed her holding herself slightly at a distance, making occasional comments about how out of the ordinary this was. It was out of the ordinary all right, but I sensed she and I were interpreting that differently.

I needed to be here for three more days. The evening before she was due to leave, I asked her to attend a dinner function at the conference with me. She readily agreed, especially after I told her Darren and his wife would be there.

We had spent some more time over at their place, and I knew she was considering making arrangements for Chocolate to be flown to stay with her in Seattle. She adored him, and I had to admit seeing her with him never failed to make me smile.

I glanced to my side where we sat at a round table with Darren and his wife and two more couples, both business partners of mine. Ellie's glossy dark hair shone under the lights from above. She'd put it up tonight, with loose tendrils hanging down to frame her face. A silver pen was pushed through the knot, holding it up, tempting me to reach over and pull it out just so I could see her hair tumble loose.

She smiled slightly as she lifted her glass of wine to take a sip. I envied the wine because it got to touch her lips. Her mouth was so fucking sexy. Her pink lips were bow-shaped with a little dimple at the top that I loved to trace with my tongue.

Let's face it, I loved to trace my tongue anywhere on Ellie. She was a delectable package of sexy and sweet, and unflinchingly beautiful. Her silk blouse tempted me with what I knew was hiding behind it. It was paired with a fitted skirt that hugged her hips down to her knees. She wore those strappy sandals again, and all I could think about was bending her over, shoving her skirt up and fucking her from behind.

She made me crazy in every way possible.

When I looked away, I caught Darren watching me from across the table. A knowing smirk was on his face when our gazes met. I shrugged. He was right about how I felt about Ellie, and I didn't care if he knew it.

The business dinner was, well, business-y.

The topics were rather dry. Ellie held her own, having enough knowledge of her brother's business to comfortably interject here and there.

I was ready for dinner to be over and get Ellie all to myself. I was so hard, I didn't know if I'd make it from the elevator all the way up to our room. Most of the time, I didn't care much beyond comfort for the amenities of having enough money to have a private penthouse and a private elevator. On nights like tonight, that private elevator was a fucking godsend because it shortened the time I'd have to wait to get my hands on her.

I heard a voice over my shoulder saying my name, and I glanced back to see Wanda Dunn approaching.

Fuck. I wasn't worried about handling the situation, but I hoped Wanda picked up on my cues. Wanda wasn't quite a friend, but she was a fairly close acquaintance with benefits. We crossed paths often as she ran an app company. She was beautiful, wealthy, and had no interest in a relationship, although she did like a good time and some no-strings sex.

There was no actual arrangement between her and me. However, we had crossed paths enough there was the loose expectation that whenever we happened to be at the same conference, or in the same location, we usually had a few drinks together and capped off the night with entirely uncomplicated sex.

I rarely knew when I was going to see her, and we didn't communicate unless we saw each other. As such, I was taken off guard to see her approaching. When she stopped by the table, Ellie was in the middle of a conversation with Sarah. Luckily, we were seated together. This was a professional setting, and I wasn't draped over Ellie the way I would've preferred to be. At a glance, I didn't think it was obvious to Wanda that Ellie and I were together.

Together?

Hell, yes. Ellie is yours. If you're not together, you have no claim.

My train of thought was rather firm and demanding. The mere consideration of Ellie being with another man sent an entirely irrational bolt of jealousy through me. There was no man, but the idea of it practically drove me crazy.

Wanda stopped beside me, resting her hand on my shoulder. "Hi, Jacob," she said warmly. "I was hoping I might run into you here."

This line of dialogue was quite typical. On the surface, it was polite and meaningless, yet I knew the insinuations well. Hoping she might "run into" me meant she hoped we'd meet up later.

I glanced up just as I felt Ellie turn to look at Wanda. "Wanda, hi there," I said, keeping my voice completely level. It wasn't Wanda's presence that sent worry spinning inside of me. Rather, it was how Ellie might interpret her. "How are you?"

Whatever undercurrents were floating under the surface between Ellie and me, it appeared Wanda didn't pick up on them. But then, why would she? For the last year or more, every time we ran into each other, we had a night together.

"I'm well. I was hoping you might be free for drinks tonight," Wanda replied.

I met her gaze, wishing I could say aloud what was tumbling through my thoughts. *Absolutely not. I'm with Ellie. And I always will be. I just have to convince her.*

Instead, I said, "Thanks for the invite, but I'll have to pass."

I didn't even care to try to keep the situation unclear. I reached for Ellie and slipped my arm around her shoulders. I didn't miss the fine thread of tension running through her.

I was kind of amazed at how quickly and

easily I felt this certain about her. It might've only been three nights, but I felt as if I knew her in a way I had never known anyone.

Wanda's eyes shifted away from my face to where my arm now rested across Ellie's shoulders. She kept her expression controlled, but I saw the flicker of surprise in her gaze.

"Of course," she said smoothly. "It's been a while since we had a chance to talk business. It was good to see you." She looked over to Darren quickly and nodded toward the other couples before departing our table.

In the brief moment with Wanda's presence there, Ellie's tension didn't dissipate. In fact, I could feel her shoulders becoming stiffer. I wasn't much for talking about feelings. Yet, I didn't expect to have feelings I needed to discuss.

Just now though, I wished I had time to explain so much to Ellie. That I'd been living half a life. That I kept all of my relationships superficial, except for a few key friendships.

I wanted to tell her that Wanda wasn't important and had never even come close to touching my heart. Not at all. I considered her a professional friend and nothing more. But I couldn't exactly say any of that right here at the table, surrounded by people.

Dinner continued, and with each passing moment, I became more restless. Usually, I was focused. Not so tonight. Ellie didn't put any physical distance between us, but I could feel the invisible distance growing and could almost sense her putting up walls around herself.

Blessedly, the function eventually ended, and we departed. I wanted to throw Ellie over my shoulder and run out of the dining room. But that wouldn't do.

Once we were in the elevator, I turned to face her, catching one of her hands in mine and sliding the other down her side. "What is it?" I asked.

"What do you mean?" she returned.

I searched her eyes, seeing the slightly guarded quality there. "I mean, ever since Wanda came over to say hello, you've been tense. She means nothing to me. She's not important."

I didn't care to get into much detail about Wanda, because it was senseless to try to pretend I didn't have some sort of past. I'd done my share of dating, usually keeping it superficial with no exceptions to that.

Ellie appeared slightly surprised I brought it up that quickly. "Who is she to you?" she asked.

"Primarily a professional acquaintance. I won't lie. We have had what might be best described as an unspoken arrangement. Sometimes when we see each other, we have drinks and so on."

Ellie caught her bottom lip in her teeth, worrying it and making me want to kiss her. Yet, I had enough sense to know now wasn't the time for that.

"Is that what we are?" she asked next, completely throwing me off.

I was prepared for questions about Wanda and, frankly, anything in my past. I wasn't prepared for questions about us.

"*No.*" My answer came out more sharply than I intended, but it was what it was. "You are far from that. You mean a lot to me," I heard myself saying, casually stumbling onto the field of a conversation for which I was entirely unprepared.

Ellie's cheeks flushed, and she kept worrying her lip, her foot starting to tap on the floor. I slid my hand over the curve of her shoulder in an unconscious attempt to soothe her anxiety. I could practically feel her vibrating.

"I don't know what's happening," she blurted out, the flush on her cheeks deepening, and her eyes showed distress as her throat worked with a swallow.

Fuck. I knew what I felt, but I hadn't put it into words, not even in my own mind.

I stepped closer, releasing her hand to lift mine and brush her silky hair away from her face, lightly cupping the side of her neck, my thumb brushing across the wild flutter of her pulse.

"I'm not sure I do either," I finally said. "But I know this is something. It's not the kind of thing I can walk away from."

Ellie stared at me, a hint of panic entering her gaze. I didn't know what to do—much less, what to say—to soothe her anxieties. So, I did the only thing I could. Bending low, I kissed her. Because whenever we touched, everything felt right.

She was stiff for a moment, a tremor running through her body. Then, she sighed, her mouth opening under mine. It felt as if she were surrendering, not to me, but to *us*, to the force between us that was alive and more potent than any words could explain.

Chapter Sixteen

JACOB

The following morning, I woke with Ellie beside me. Last night had taken us to the same edge as before, rough and wild, leaving us spent in the aftermath of a storm of sensation.

This morning was no different. Her sweet bottom was pressed against my already aching arousal. I found one of her lush breasts with my hand and dropped kisses along the downy skin of her neck.

Once again, I sank into her channel and thought maybe, just maybe, I was the luckiest fucking man in the world.

A few hours later, I had work to do. I was deep into an online chat with Darren as we sorted out a separate tech issue at two of his hotel systems. We were running a few beta projects—small ones, so we could target them to sort out the bugs.

Ellie had gone out to do some shopping. She kissed me goodbye this morning, and I had sensed the reserve in her. I hoped whatever shadow Wanda's brief appearance had cast had already dissipated.

Later that afternoon, when she didn't reply to my texts, I returned to the hotel suite to find she hadn't returned. My gut pinged. Something felt off. A quick look around, and I found no sign of her clothes. My eyes snagged on a single sheet of paper on the dresser. She was gone. She left me a fucking note.

I was conflicted inside, anger tangling with a sense of feeling bereft. I was used to being in control of myself and of situations. This felt entirely out of my control.

On a single sheet of white paper, she wrote,

Jacob, the last few days have been incredible and unexpected. I was going to tell you what time my flight left today, but then I thought it best that I didn't. I know neither one of us planned on this, so perhaps it's best to leave it just as it is. It's perfect, and I don't want to sully it with expectations.

I don't know if you picked up on this, but I'm a

bit of a wishful thinker. I'm not nearly as clear-headed and logical as my brother, who you've known longer than me.

I might not have known you that long, but I sense you're more like him. In reality, I think we both know you're a little bit out of my league, so to speak. I'd like to remember this for what it was.

Incredible.

xoxo

Ellie

PS: I've arranged for Chocolate to be flown up to Seattle. For me, he'll always remind me of you a little bit because without meeting you, I wouldn't have met him.

I kept rereading her note as if somehow the words would change, and I would realize I misunderstood what she was saying.

After about the fourth time, my hand fell as I clenched the piece of paper.

"No," I said to the room.

Only once before had I felt this helpless. When my sister died. That kind of pain was more terrifying and brutal. But it had the same undertone to it, a sense of something I needed to fix and didn't know how.

I strolled across the suite, snatching my phone off the bar where I set it when I paused to pour myself a whiskey. Swiping the screen with my thumb, I tapped Darren's number.

"What's up?" he asked by way of greeting.

"Put Sarah on."

Darren laughed. "Dude, of course you can talk to Sarah, but what's up? You sound a little off."

"Is Ellie there?" I asked, distantly noticing my tone sounded panicked.

"Uh, no. She's not. I know she stopped by earlier to take care of some paperwork since she's adopting Chocolate. Sarah is ecstatic about that, by the way. Sarah took her to the airport. I thought you knew she was leaving."

"Fuck."

"So, let me get this straight. While you were busy working today, she left and you didn't know that was happening. Am I right?" he asked, the understanding evident in his tone annoying me.

"Yes," I muttered. "Can you find out what time her flight left?"

His voice was muffled when he moved the phone away from his mouth. "Sarah! What time did you drop Ellie off today?" There was a moment of silence, and then, "Okay, thanks."

His voice returned to the phone. "Sarah

said her flight left hours ago. She should be landing in Seattle anytime now because Sarah said it was a direct flight."

"All right. I'm gonna have to cancel our plans to do a little more work tomorrow."

Darren chuckled. "Fine with me. I take it you're going after Ellie."

"Damn straight."

"Have you told her how you feel?" he asked, his tone sobering.

I bit back my anger. Because I wanted to tell him to fuck off. "No," I finally said.

"Well then, you might want to do something about that."

———

With Darren's words echoing in my mind, I rushed to get back to Seattle. Unfortunately, nothing happened as fast as I wanted. I found myself in the unenviable position of making vague excuses to a number of business contacts as I canceled meetings in my rush to return to Seattle.

Maybe I hadn't planned on Ellie, maybe I hadn't planned on ever letting anyone into my heart again, yet the idea of letting our weekend be nothing more than that wasn't something I was willing to live with. I wanted Ellie every day.

My pride wanted to chalk it up to incredible sex. And it *was* absolutely *incredible*. Yet, that wasn't what had me tied up in knots inside, with cold fear sliding through my veins and settling like an icy knot around my heart.

I was missing Ellie's pure heart, the light and air she injected into my life like a warm summer breeze after months of cold, dark winter. In the midst of all my calls as I scrambled to arrange my abrupt departure, I reflexively answered the phone, not checking to see who was calling.

"Jacob!" my father's voice boomed through the line.

"Oh, hey, Dad. I wasn't expecting a call from you."

"Of course you weren't," he replied with a chuckle. "It's all business for you, son. I'm just calling to let you know your mother is going in tomorrow for an unexpected procedure." His tone shifted from jovial to somber in a flash. "She'll be fine."

That fear around my heart squeezed, an icy fist of dread.

"What do you mean, Dad? A procedure?"

"Don't you panic. It's all I can do to keep my shit together," he said bluntly. "She went in for a regular appointment earlier this week, and they found a shadow in one of her breast scans."

I leaned against the wall beside the bed in my hotel suite, which felt cavernous and echoing without Ellie's presence. Resting my head against the wall, I took a breath. "How do you know she's going to be okay?" I asked.

"Because she says so," he said, and I could hear the emotion in his voice.

My parents were one of the lucky couples, or that's what I told myself. They were still quite happily married, and my father adored my mother.

"I'm coming home early, so I'll be there tomorrow."

"You are?" my dad asked, his tone genuinely surprised.

"I am. Before you ask, I'm chasing after a girl," I said, my own laugh disbelieving.

My father was dead silent before he let out a sharp bark of a laugh. "I'll be damned. A girl got to you. I can't wait to meet her."

My heart was thudding against my ribs, too hard to consider what was on the line. "I'm glad I'm already on the way, so I can be there for you and Mom. I'll call tomorrow?"

"I'll call you as soon as we know something. Your mother would love to see you.

She won't want you to come to the appointment though."

Minutes later, I hung up the phone, frozen in place for a few beats. The combination of this abrupt concern for my mother, who had already survived breast cancer once, tangling up with the situation with Ellie left me feeling off-balance.

There was a reason why I preferred not to get emotionally involved. I knew the feeling of loss—brutal loss—too well. Yet, something about Ellie had broken down all the walls around my heart and overrode all of my common sense.

With a muttered curse, I pushed away from the wall and swiftly finished packing, practically running out of the hotel.

Chapter Seventeen

ELLIE

I idly stirred my mug of hot chocolate. My flight had landed yesterday evening. As planned, Chocolate had arrived this morning. He was presently curled up in a corner of the couch, after sniffing my entire apartment quite thoroughly. Between the rescues I fostered on occasion and Sally's presence here before she passed away, I was certain his nose had been working overtime. After Chocolate had his fill of smelling everything, he'd happily chowed down on a bowl of food, lapped at his water, and then curled up to fall into a deep sleep.

Last night, I had plenty to do to keep my mind somewhat occupied. I had rushed out to get new supplies just for him, including a brand-new dog bed, a bowl, and a bright purple collar and leash. I was *that* kind of dog person. I got them everything. If they let me, I put sweaters on them when it was cold. I had no shame.

I had taken Chocolate out this morning in the cool, misty rain. Now, we were back at my apartment, and I was bored and lonely and missing Jacob.

I usually liked the flexibility of working for myself. I didn't answer to anyone other than my customers, and I did that on my schedule. Because I had known this trip was coming, way back when Wayne and I first planned it, I had everything lined out. I didn't need to rush and start working on any projects. It wasn't until next week that I had a few shows to prep for. In my normal world, I liked having a few days when I came back from being out of town to settle into my routine and regain my bearings.

After the glitter and glamour of Las Vegas, the unexpected blackout, and then those incredibly hot days and nights with Jacob, I was restless and doing my damnedest to ignore the lingering ache in my heart.

Chocolate was the only bright spot, and he was a sweetie—all soft, warm, snuggly, and friendly. I was ready for my own dog again. I could start fostering again now. It seemed a little insane, but I couldn't foster when I didn't have my own dog. I wanted to keep them all, so it was best I wasn't tempted to do that.

After Sally passed away, I checked the local shelter occasionally, but I hadn't felt quite ready. Chocolate let me know I was ready.

During our walk, I had taken him to the dog park for him to play with other dogs, and tossed a ball for him to fetch for a bit. We both got drenched because it was Seattle in January, and it rained here a lot.

I looked around my small apartment and sighed. I lived in an upstairs apartment in a neighborhood close to downtown Seattle. My apartment wasn't big or fancy, but it was comfortable. It was nothing to compare to where I imagined Jacob lived. I kept mentally ordering myself not to be curious, but my mind was steadfastly ignoring me. It was like a little puppy scampering about, sniffing at every possible train of thought that involved Jacob. I couldn't help it. Dog metaphors came easily to me.

My apartment should have been a firm reminder of why Jacob and I were not meant to be. It was the upstairs of one of those cute

little bungalow-style houses. In the spring
and summer, I had flower boxes in the windows, little splashes of color to cheer me up.

The front windows looked out over the
street. A wash of raindrops rolling down over
the windowpanes blurred the view. Hardwood floors stretched across the main room
where you entered from the side door to the
stairs outside. It had an angled roof, creating
the sense of a larger space when it really was
tiny. The kitchen and living room were one
open room. The only thing demarcating the
kitchen from the living room was the shift
from hardwood floors to tile. I had put a
table in between the spaces, which kind of
behaved like an island, but not really. The
kitchen was tucked into the corner with two
counters along the walls. It was perfect for
one person.

To the back, there was just one bedroom
and a bathroom. The entire space was cozy,
decorated with my usual haphazard, quirky
flair. My latest focus with my art was fabric
wall hangings and quilts. I had two hanging
on the walls to brighten the space, along with
a deep purple woven rug in the center of the
living room. A sectional sofa and a coffee table, along with two end tables, were the extent of the furnishings.

It was entirely unglamorous and nothing like what I imagined Jacob was accustomed to. I wasn't one to hold myself up to others like a yardstick, not usually. I preferred to just be who I was. Because anything else was too disheartening.

Yet, I couldn't help but think of how easily Jacob had intervened in my potentially disastrous hotel room situation in Las Vegas. It wasn't as if he needed to spend money to solve the problem. He could have, and it wouldn't have been any trouble for him. Whereas, if I had been in the position where I had to use one of my credit cards to cover an unexpected room cost, it probably would've taken me months and months and months to pay it off, if I was lucky.

I usually thought things through. It wasn't that it never crossed my mind that Wayne might try to use that room, but I was stubborn about it. I told myself it would all work out for the best, and he didn't deserve it.

Fucking Wayne and Cheryl. I'd learned a bruising lesson about where to place my trust.

With a sigh, I sipped my hot chocolate and added a dash of cream liqueur from the cabinet. Stepping away from the counter, I padded into the living room to sink onto the couch beside Chocolate. I rubbed his fur lightly. It was still slightly damp, but it was drying and willy-nilly curls were forming all over his back. I smiled, dipping my head to press a kiss to his forehead. He let out a soft sigh as he sank more deeply into the couch.

When I left that note for Jacob, I thought it made perfect sense. Oh, I hadn't wanted to write it. But I could be foolish. I had gotten jealous when that woman approached him the night before. My reaction had been a timely reminder of what I needed to remember.

Namely, that Jacob's world was different from mine. Glamorous, confident women who could do the whole acquaintances-with-benefits thing with style fit into his world better than I did. My stupid heart, my oh-so-foolish heart, had started to spin fantasies around us.

That was dangerous.

Staring out into the rainy view, I curled my feet under my knees. I had dressed in my absolute most comfortable clothes—my favorite pair of fleece sweatpants and a loose fleece top. With no bra, of course, because I was home alone, and it didn't matter. To finish it off, I was wearing a pair of fuzzy pink socks.

I was warm, dry, and comfortable. The cold winter rain falling outside was held at bay. I might be a little lonely, and I might be longing for Jacob, but I was fine. Totally fine.

I took a sip of my now spiked hot chocolate and leaned back into the cushions, reaching for the remote just as there was a sharp knock at my door.

Chocolate lifted his head and let out a soft bark, his eyes looking to me. Having had rescues and fosters many times, I sensed he was trying to assess what I wanted him to do. I definitely wanted him to let me know when anybody came to the door, so I reached over and stroked across the top of his head, scratching gently as I praised him.

Who would be showing up at my place now?

I set my mug on the coffee table and stood to walk to the door. I hesitated for a moment. I didn't look bad, but I also didn't usually invite company over when I was in my most comfortable clothes. With a shrug, I kept walking. Probably a delivery, or something.

Chapter Eighteen

ELLIE

Chocolate followed me over to the door, a low rumble coming from his throat.

Leaning forward to look through the peephole in the door, I was stunned to see Jacob on the other side. His eyes were cast down and the lines of tension evident on his face.

My breath caught in my throat, and my heart started pounding, echoing through my body as blood rushed in my ears. I opened the door slowly.

I stood there silently, frozen, although the inside of my body was going wild. Chocolate instantly recognized Jacob and started wagging madly, circling Jacob's legs and dashing in and out of the door.

Jacob and I simply stared at each other. He looked weary, his eyes containing a slightly wild look. He was a far cry from the polished man I was accustomed to seeing. He leaned his hands on either side of the doorframe, almost as if he needed something to hold onto.

"Ellie," he finally said, his voice raspy.

"Jacob, I..."

Just as I managed to actually speak, a squirrel leapt from a nearby tree onto the deck railing. Chocolate let out a quick bark and dashed through the door and down the steps.

Jacob moved, reflexively looking toward Chocolate. I started to race after him, and Jacob was right ahead of me. Blessedly, the yard was fenced, but I couldn't even remember if I had thought to close the gate behind me when we came in earlier.

With a quick call from Jacob, and the squirrel wisely finding another tree to hide in, Chocolate lost interest and trotted to Jacob's side at the bottom of the stairs. I waited by the door as they returned.

Perhaps, to some people, Jacob's instinct to instantly go after Chocolate would seem like a small thing. To me, it meant everything. He didn't think it was silly that I would worry about Chocolate racing off, he didn't care about the rain. He knew it would matter to me that Chocolate was safe and sound, so he got him right away.

With my heart still thudding wildly, I paused to check on Chocolate, the distraction a bit of a relief. "I see you chase squirrels," I said, as I leaned over and ran my hand along his damp back. I wasn't in the mood to tell him he shouldn't.

Tail wagging, Chocolate trotted back into the warm, dry apartment. Jacob and I stood there, staring at each other in the rain.

"Thanks for getting him," I said, swiping a raindrop out of my eye.

That electricity that seemed to hover around us whenever we were near each other started humming. Jacob stepped closer to me.

"We can talk in a minute," he murmured, right before he pulled me close and brushed his lips across mine.

He smelled like rain and Jacob, and his mouth was so warm. His kiss was quick, but it was oh-so-good. His lips molded themselves to mine, his tongue tracing along the seam before sweeping in. When he drew away, he dropped kisses on each corner of my mouth. I was nearly breathless from it.

"You're cold," he said softly, his hand running down my back in a smooth pass over my now wet and almost soggy clothes. "Let's get inside."

I was shivering, and I was a bit stunned. My body was spinning like a top, and my heart was frantically doing cartwheels in my chest.

With a nudge on my shoulder, Jacob caught my hand in his and led me through the door, closing it behind us.

"I don't suppose I could borrow a towel," he said, his eyelashes glittering with raindrops.

"Of course," I replied.

My socks, which had been warm and fuzzy moments earlier, made a squishy sound as I walked across the living room into the bathroom and fetched three towels.

Handing one to Jacob and hanging the other over the back of a chair to dry Chocolate in a moment, I glanced to him. "I'm going to change. Be right back."

Stepping into my bedroom, I quickly stripped out of my wet clothes and yanked on another pair of fleece sweatpants and top. This time, I made do with a pair of blue cotton socks. When I returned, I looked over to see Jacob toweling Chocolate off, who appeared to view it as a form of petting.

My heart gave a swift kick. Jacob wasn't supposed to show up like this. My willpower was faltering. Badly.

He straightened, casting a grin in my direction. "He's as dry as he's going to get with a towel. But he likes it, so..."

He shrugged, and I couldn't help but return his grin. "I wish I had something that fit you."

My eyes practically ate up the way his T-shirt clung to his chest. He'd shrugged out of his jacket and now his navy T-shirt was the only thing between me and his delicious body. Well, that and his jeans.

Of course, that's what I wanted. I tried to remind myself we didn't make sense. Perhaps when we were naked, and he was buried inside of me. Then, everything felt right. But sex wasn't real life.

Chocolate trotted across the room, returning to the couch to curl up on the towel I had laid out for him there earlier. His soft sigh was the only sound in the quiet room.

Jacob held the towel in his hands, looking at me across the roughly four feet that separated us. For a moment, I saw uncertainty flicker in his gaze. His shoulders rose and fell with a deep breath, but he never once looked away from me. When he spoke, his words came out slow and deliberate.

"Here's the thing. I don't really know how to do this. My sister died. We were very close, and it nearly killed me. Not literally, obviously. I guess I decided I didn't want anyone to matter that much. Until I met you, it was easy. Now, the only thing that's easy is being with you. Maybe it's crazy because it's only been days, but I think I love you."

He went quiet, while my heart practically broke a rib. Before I realized it, he dropped the towel on the floor and closed the distance between us in two long strides. He was wiping away my tears with his thumb as he asked, "What's wrong?"

I hadn't even realized I started to cry. I wasn't sad, just overwhelmed with emotion. It was slamming through me so hard, I could hardly think. All I could do was feel. My mind thought it was crazy and wanted to argue the point. All the while, my heart knew.

Because I knew how I felt when I was with Jacob. *Exactly* right. There was a raw honesty and intimacy between us.

I shook my head, swallowing through the emotion tightening my throat. "I'm not sad, just overwhelmed. I wrote that note and got on the plane, and then kind of fell apart. My mind tells me one thing..."

My words stopped when Jacob stepped a bit closer again, this time pulling me into his arms, his hand brushing my tangled, wet hair away from my face.

"I don't care what your mind says, or mine," he said gruffly.

That was always the way it was with him. It didn't seem to matter how short a time we'd been together—the moment I was held close in Jacob's embrace, I felt right. My heartbeat kept on pounding, drumming a dance of joy.

Staring into his ebullient gaze, I took a breath and let it out, the sharp ache of missing him unspooling inside. "Okay," I said softly, feeling my lips curl into a smile.

Once again, his mouth was on mine, and I tumbled into the fire of need and intimacy. I needn't have bothered with changing because Jacob made quick work of my clothes.

We left a scattered trail of clothes through the living room with Jacob maneuvering me in the bedroom. My skin was cool and hot, all at once, chilled from the rain and burning hot from the fire Jacob set alight inside of me.

As I turned to kick my pants off, my feet

tangled and I stumbled, catching my balance when my palms fell onto the mattress at the foot of my bed. Jacob didn't miss a beat.

He never missed a beat.

Not with me, and not with us.

I was already soaking wet, my arousal slick on the insides of my thighs. That was how easily he affected me. A few kisses, and I was nearly out of my mind for him.

I started to turn, but his other hand slid down my spine, a hot brand on my skin. His lips pressed against the curve of my bottom, his fingers teasing between my thighs. I moaned, arching back and flexing into his touch.

His hand left me, and I heard him murmur, "You taste so fucking good."

Glancing over my shoulder, I caught sight of him drawing his fingers out of his mouth. My pussy clenched, and I closed my eyes when a sharp burst of pleasure hit me as he brought his hand back between my thighs, his thumb circling my clit before he buried his fingers in my channel.

Pressure was spinning inside of me, my release already barreling toward me. He buried his face between my thighs from behind, his tongue licking through my folds as he fucked me with his fingers.

It was quick and fast, a deep drive as he stretched my channel and sucked my clit lightly. Pleasure burst through me like firecrackers, my entire body lighting up and my nerves sizzling. Pleasure blurred to an intensity that was almost painful as I shuddered.

Before I could even catch my breath, as the aftershocks of my climax rippled through me, I felt Jacob rise up, and the head of his cock press at my entrance. There was a slow slide into my channel as I was still throbbing and pulsing.

He held still once he was buried inside of me, murmuring my name. Then, he drew out swiftly, spinning me around, onto my back on the mattress. His weight slowly came down over me as he settled in the cradle of my hips. His hands brushed my hair away from my face, and I opened my eyes, colliding with the heat of his gaze.

"I needed to see you," he said, just as he sheathed himself inside of me, filling me to the hilt instantly.

My body reacted, my legs curling around him, welcoming him into me. Once again, he held still for a beat before he began to pull back and rock into me. My hips bucked into him reflexively.

I couldn't even speak. He dusted kisses at

the corners of my mouth as he eased back. Another slow slide into me. The slick fusion of our joining was so intoxicating, it nearly toppled me over the edge. He sank into me deeply once more, creating just enough friction against my highly sensitized, swollen clit that I went flying instantly.

I came in a rough cry. He caught it in our kiss, as he went taut, the heat of his release filling me in a last driving surge.

Chapter Nineteen

JACOB

I was tangled up in Ellie, skin to skin, my heart beating so hard and fast, I could hardly catch my breath. Much less think past the intense storm of sensation, need, and intimacy. I rolled to my side, holding her close.

After a few moments, as I felt the *thud* of her heart beating in tune with mine, I managed to take a breath. Leaning back slightly, I adjusted the pillows behind me and glanced down to her. Her head was resting against my shoulder, her dark hair a tangled mess around her face, still damp from our few minutes outside in the rain.

I had no idea what time it was. I didn't even care. I was beyond relieved to be here.

She opened her eyes, and my heart

squeezed. Thank fuck she hadn't turned me away.

"Hey," I said softly.

A smile slowly stretched across her face, and she leaned up on an elbow to press her lips to mine before drawing back quickly.

"You're here," she said, her tone wondering.

"I am," I replied with a chuckle. "And I'm not going anywhere today. It sucks outside."

Ellie giggled, the sound spinning around my heart.

At that moment, Chocolate jumped onto the foot of her bed and stepped between our legs, promptly settling down with a big sigh.

Ellie laughed. "I haven't decided if he should be allowed on the bed yet. Thanks for going out to get him earlier."

"Of course. I figured this is a new place for him. You don't need him running off."

She was quiet for a moment, her eyes suddenly bright. "It says everything."

Puzzled, I arched a brow in question.

"You *get* me, and you know what matters. That's all." She leaned forward to kiss me again. "Do you want some hot chocolate?"

"I'd love some hot chocolate. I'm starving too. Mind if I order some pizza to be delivered?"

Ellie grinned. "Of course not."

That's how it turned out I spent a rainy evening and night with Ellie. I rarely took time off. Even when I didn't have official business to do, in my spare time, I was usually working on some kind of project related to it. An evening when all I did was lounge on the couch with my girl and a sweet dog was as rare as an actual diamond in the sky.

The following morning, her phone chirped on the kitchen table where we were seated. Ellie glanced at the screen and then up to me, her coffee cup halfway to her mouth before she lowered it. "It's Aidan. Do you want to talk to him?"

"Yes. You're important to me. I'd rather have this conversation with him before he gets pissed off at me because he finds out about us some other way."

"What about me? And how I feel? I don't answer to my brother."

"I know you don't. If you want to be the first to tell him, go right ahead. I don't see how we can keep this a secret, and I don't want to. You're not a fling. You're mine," I said flatly.

For a moment, it looked as if Ellie wanted to be pissed off at me. But then she leaned across the counter and kissed me, fast and fierce.

"How about I call him back and tell him you have something to tell him. Because I kind of want to freak him out a little bit," she said with a sly grin.

"Totally fine with me."

Chapter Twenty

JACOB

A few days later, I waited outside Aidan's door. We were meeting Aidan and his wife, Becca, for dinner, and Ellie had arrived here ahead of me. I'd spent the afternoon with my parents. My mother was fine. Blessedly, the follow-up tests revealed a buildup of scar tissue, but no new signs of cancer. Between that and facing up to my feelings for Ellie, well, it had been an emotional few days. My years-long vow to never care too much for anyone had officially gone up in smoke.

Aidan and I already had words. Twice. The first time was when I called him with Ellie.

He kept himself in check then, if only because Ellie was right there and interrupted several times to take the phone from me and tell Aidan he had no say in her love life. The second time was the following day, when I received a cryptic text from him.

Meet me at my office.

Although his text was brief and to the point, I knew damn well it had nothing to do with our usual collaborative work. I wasn't one for taking orders, but I hadn't hesitated to agree. It was personal for him, and I knew it.

The offices for his security company were below where he and Becca lived in a nondescript warehouse-style building in downtown Seattle. The outside of the building gave no clues to how glamorous it was on the inside.

When I met with Aidan, he had made it perfectly clear he was fucking pissed at me for making a move on his sister. I think he would've liked to haul off and punch me, but once again, Ellie kept him in check. Apparently, she'd called him before I arrived, to preemptively chew him out if he dared lay a hand on me. According to him, he held off out of respect for her.

I made it plainly clear how I felt about Ellie. I wasn't sure if that's what persuaded him to calm down. Perhaps it was Becca, who arrived while we were talking and told him to back the hell off.

I surmised tonight was supposed to be a peace offering orchestrated by Becca. When I knocked on the door, it swung open a moment later. Aidan stood there, tall, dark, and inscrutable. His hair was darker than Ellie's and his eyes were blue to her hazel, yet they were clearly related. He was an easy fit for working in security as a former Navy SEAL with a naturally forbidding presence and acute awareness. He was also a genius with coding and other tech issues, so he was a pleasure to work with.

"Jacob," he said with a quick nod before stepping back and letting me pass through the door.

I was immediately bombarded by Chocolate and Oscar, Aidan and Becca's dog. Ellie had explained to me Oscar had come to Aidan via a foster stay with her. The two dogs appeared to be getting along famously. Oscar's black tail bumped against my legs as he circled me in greeting, with Chocolate following behind him.

After petting the dogs, I glanced up to find Ellie standing right there, a smile playing at the corners of her mouth. Aidan was a close audience, and I didn't forget it. She caught my hand in hers and leaned up to press a kiss on my cheek. It took all of my restraint not to turn and pull her into a full body kiss. But I had *some* sense.

Aidan's alert gaze bounced between us before Becca's voice broke into the moment. "Come on over, Jacob," she called.

I wouldn't quite call where they lived an apartment. It was as large as a house and comprised most of the upstairs of Aidan's security company building. It had an industrial feel to it, but it was much softer and warmer ever since Becca moved in a few years ago.

With dark hardwood floors spanning the entire space and exposed piping painted neutral colors above, the space felt open and airy. Becca had softened the feel with curtains in the windows and brightly colored rugs scattered about. She was in the kitchen at the far end of the main room, which was separated from the living room space by an oval shaped counter.

With Ellie holding my hand firmly, we walked across the room. Becca, with her glossy brown hair and bright blue eyes, was lovely and a perfect counterpart for Aidan. She also completely ignored his tendency to be overprotective. She rounded the counter to throw her arms around me.

"I haven't seen you in months. Then I hear from Ellie that you two went and fell in love in Las Vegas during the blackout. That is *so* romantic," she said with a smile as she stepped back, looking to Aidan, who appeared to be under orders to behave.

He rolled his eyes and smiled. "Don't make me say it's romantic."

Becca laughed as she stepped to his side, tugging him down to her for a quick kiss. Aidan seemed to relax.

"Where's little Aidan?" I asked, after Becca directed us over to a round dining room table adjacent to the kitchen.

She poured wine for all of us and set out an appetizer tray of cheese and bread. "He spent the day with my parents in Bellingham, so he's sound asleep. They dropped him off about an hour ago. Don't worry," she said, gesturing to the baby monitor sitting in the center of the dining room table, "we'll hear if he wakes up. I think I've got the most elaborate baby monitor setup in the world.

"If you ever have kids, I bet you'll be just as bad. We'll give you our system because I can't handle another baby. There are cameras everywhere. I told Aidan I hate it because I feel like I'm being watched. Then, he told me to go without it for a day, and I thought I was going to go crazy. I don't know how people had babies before modern technology."

"I think they swaddled them to their chest at all times," Ellie offered with a laugh.

Becca chuckled and got up to check on the lasagna she had in the oven. Dinner moved along, and I found—just as with everything with Ellie—this just felt right. I knew she and Aidan were close. I'd known that before our unexpected and life-altering weekend in Vegas.

It simply felt right when I was with her, no matter the situation. It wasn't that I wasn't a social man. It was more that my life had narrowed to one focus—work. It had been several years since I'd done anything with anyone where it wasn't for purposes of business.

As dinner wound down, Ellie went with Becca to check on little Aidan, and I found myself alone at the table with Aidan. He looked over at me, his gaze considering. I sensed he had something to say, so I stayed quiet.

He spun his empty wineglass between his fingers and let out a sigh. "I'm still a little cranky about it, but you're really important to Ellie. It seems like she really matters to you," he said quietly, then paused, his gaze narrowing. "If you hurt a single fucking hair on her head, let's just say, it won't be a friendly conversation."

I completely respected Aidan. I also knew Ellie answered only for herself and not to her brother. Yet, my sister had ended up dead, so to say I understood his concern didn't quite cut how thoroughly I comprehended it.

I held Aidan's gaze and nodded slowly. "I absolutely understand. I can promise you I won't hurt her. In any way."

Something about this conversation solidified the depth of my feelings for Ellie, but I wasn't about to discuss that with Aidan. Her voice drifted to us as she returned from the baby's bedroom, with Becca walking behind her.

I reflexively glanced in her direction. She walked toward us, her cheeks a little flushed and her eyes bright. My heart gave a resounding *thump*.

EPILOGUE

Ellie

About six months later

The lights glittered above as I laid down my cards. I was back in Vegas. The power was most definitely *on*.

I felt a warm touch on my thigh. Jacob's palm coasted over the smooth surface of my skirt to the hem. I was instantly distracted and glanced to him. His eyes caught mine, the lights glinting off his dark hair. There was a wicked gleam in his gaze, and it made me squirm in my seat.

"What are you doing?" I hissed under my breath.

Jacob leaned over, his breath teasing my

ear and sending prickles over the surface of my skin. "Making you crazy," he murmured, right before his palm coasted under my skirt and his fingers teased between my thighs.

Dear God.

This man.

He knew how to make me crazy.

I studiously looked away. I mean, I was in the middle of gambling. I needed to focus.

In the six months or so that had passed since our last trip here, things had moved quickly with us. If it didn't feel so incredibly right, I might've started to panic.

When my lease came up on my apartment a few months ago, Jacob cajoled me into moving in with him. Not that he had to try too hard. We spent every night together as it was. Of course, his place was much nicer, and I tried to protest. He silenced me with kiss after kiss after kiss, telling me he loved me, and it wasn't about his place being better, it was because we belonged together.

You try saying no to that.

Of course, I loved him. So much it hurt sometimes.

With him teasing the damp silk between my thighs, I forfeited the game and we left.

The private elevator to our penthouse suite was beginning to feel like our own personal sex playground. On the way up, he sent me flying with his fingers before we stumbled through the door.

The sex between us was amazing, and I was beginning to wonder if it would ever fade. But that wasn't what made me love Jacob so much. It was his solid, steady affection, the way he was with Chocolate and every rescue I brought to his much nicer place than mine.

It was the look in his eyes, and how he made me dinner when I was tired. It was how he made me feel more protected and more secure than I had ever felt in my life.

It was how I occasionally saw the glimmers of vulnerability in his eyes and knew it was a leap of faith every time he let his heart stay open to me. Because that's what love was, every single day. Trying again and getting past the fear.

———

JACOB

No one ever did find out what caused the blackout during the time when our paths fatefully crossed in Las Vegas. Aidan and I did a lot of digging on our own, along with others we were affiliated with in the security world. We were able to pin down a hack as the cause, but not who was responsible.

It still bothered me. I liked answers, and I didn't like it when I couldn't find them. I was still grateful the power had gone out. I don't know what would've happened if it hadn't. It tilted my world sideways with Ellie and pushed us both to drop our guards in ways we might not have otherwise.

I woke up beside her in Vegas. She was warm and burrowed against my side. Her preferred way of sleeping was with her head tucked against my shoulder and one of her feet between my calves. I didn't mind one bit.

I usually woke up with my hand cupping her sweet ass, and this morning was no exception. I also usually preferred to dally and tease her to madness before we got out of bed.

Today, however, I had plans.

As much as I wanted to stay in bed beside her, I had another priority. I eased away from her, praying she would stay asleep, and breathed a sigh of relief when she did. Once I was up, I called down to the main desk. Within minutes, the ring I had looked for high and low for her was delivered.

Ellie was an artist. Getting her the per-

fect ring wasn't about money, or a big diamond. Not at all. It was about finding the
exact right thing that was *just* for her and, of
course, custom-made.

I had talked to Aidan, Becca, and even
some of her close friends in my search. I
eventually chased down a jeweler she loved in
Vancouver, British Columbia. It had required
my passport and several personal visits to
hammer out the design. After all of that, I'd
had it delivered here. Vegas was meaningful
to me due to what it represented with regard
to Ellie, who held my heart in her hands.

Every. Single. Day.

After the ring was delivered, I inspected
it at the counter once again. It was a plat-
inum band set with an amethyst, her favorite
stone. It was simple, elegant and perfect.

After that, I started coffee and ordered
room service for breakfast. I was restless for
Ellie to wake up. She was usually an early
riser, as I was. Yet this morning, I didn't expect her up as early because we had stayed
out late the night before. It was Vegas when
night became day.

Blessedly, I didn't have to wait long. She
came wandering out of the bedroom, wearing
my button-down shirt, which hung halfway
down her thighs. With her hair a tousled

mess and her eyes hazed with sleep, she smiled when she saw me.

"Good morning. You're up early today."

I pulled her close, bending low to press a kiss to her lips. She tasted minty. "You already brushed your teeth," I observed as I pulled back.

She shrugged. "Of course."

I was unaccountably nervous. For a man who rarely worried, my heart was thudding hard in my chest, and I was anxious for her to get her coffee. I didn't think it was best to ambush her with a marriage proposal before she was fully awake.

Just then, there was a knock at the door. She glanced over as she was adding cream to her coffee, a puzzled look on her face.

"I ordered us brunch," I explained as I strode to the door, breathing a silent sigh of relief. My plan was falling into place.

The delivery waiter wheeled the cart in after I deftly slipped the ring box under the cover for her favorite French toast. Within minutes, we were sitting down at the table, and she lifted the lid, her eyes going wide at the sight of the blue velvet box.

"Oh my God," she murmured, her eyes swinging to mine as she stared at the box. "Jacob, is this what I think it is?"

"Maybe. I know that it comes with a question."

Her eyes glistened with tears. "Go ahead, you should look first," I said, willing my pounding heart to slow, and failing.

She lifted the box gingerly, her hands shaking. When she opened it, her breath came out in a rush. "Oh. Oh my. It's beautiful."

She leapt up from her chair, racing around the small table and flinging herself in my lap. In the process, she knocked my coffee on the floor and we almost tipped over my plate.

It didn't matter. I had a bundle of Ellie in my lap and that was all that really mattered.

"Yes," she declared as she peppered my face with kisses. I felt light, lighter than I had in years.

"You didn't even give me a chance to ask."

"Oh right. Were you planning to ask me to marry you?" she asked in between kisses.

"Yes."

"Then, that's my answer. Yes." *Kiss*. "Yes." *Kiss*. "Yes." She finished off with one more kiss.

My throat was tight with emotion and my heart swelled so hard, I thought it might break through the bounds of my ribs. Tears weren't something that came for me often, but right now, my eyes were damp.

"I thought Vegas was the best place for this."

"Ooh, are we going to elope?"

I laughed, holding her close against me, feeling the beat of her heart against my chest.

"That's what I was hoping for, but I don't know if it counts as eloping when I was kind of planning on it."

I couldn't quite believe Ellie was mine.

She leaned back, sniffling a little as she wiped the tears away from her eyes with her knuckles. "Were you worried I wouldn't say yes?"

"Seeing as this is the biggest question I've ever asked anyone in my life, yes, I was a little worried."

She twisted her lips to the side and wrinkled her nose before leaning forward to press her forehead against mine. "With us, there was never any doubt."

Just us. Always.

Thank you for reading Just Us - I hope you loved Ellie & Jacob's story!

If you'd like to get the full story for Becca & Aidan, check out Just This Once. Aidan is a sexy, alpha SEAL who's been half in love with Becca for years. One night turns into so much more.

Tall, dark, sexy, and oh-so-alpha, don't miss Aidan's story!

For a look at my latest series, check out Burn For Me - a second chance romance for the ages. Sexy firefighters? Check. Rugged men? Check. Wrapped up together? Check. Brave the fire in these hot, small-town romances. Amelia & Cade were high school sweethearts & then it all fell apart. When they cross paths again, it's epic - don't miss Cade's story! It's FREE everywhere!

Keep reading for a sneak peek.

Be sure to sign up for my newsletter for the latest news, teasers & more! Click here to sign up: http://jhcroixauthor.com/subscribe/

SNEAK PEEK: BURN FOR ME

Amelia

I shoved through the door into the bar, coming to a quick stop as my eyes adjusted to the light. I brushed a wet lock of hair off of my cheek and threaded through the tables to the bar at the back. Once I slipped onto a stool, the bartender spun to face me. He was a jolly looking man with round blue eyes.

"I'm Tank. You look like you could use a drink," he announced, his wide smile softening his observation.

"A beer will do," I replied.

"House draft okay?" he asked.

At my nod, he spun around. Within seconds, he'd handed me my beer and silently offered a clean towel. Though it was tiny, seeing as it was a bar towel, I quickly scrubbed it over my dripping wet hair and face before handing it back to him. I settled in to try to forget my shitty day.

A bit later, I drained my beer and glanced around the bar, savoring the anonymity of being in a crowded bar in Anchorage, Alaska where no one knew me. I was tucked in the corner by the wall, pleased to have a nice view of the crowd and yet go unnoticed by just about everyone there. Tank caught my eyes again, a question held in them. I nodded and held my empty pint glass aloft. He nodded in return while he mixed a drink for someone and pulled another pint for me with his free hand. The extent of my conversation with anyone this evening had been limited to Tank's earlier introduction.

If he thought anything awry with the fact I was wearing a wedding dress splashed with mud, he didn't show it. Neither did anyone around me. Anchorage was just large enough of a city people left you alone if you appeared to want to be left as such. That said, people were friendly too. Alaska, despite its sprawling geography, kept its residents close, all bound by the knowledge they lived on the edge of the wild and had the strength and guts for such a life.

I took a drag on what was my third beer

and wondered if perhaps I should slow down. I was definitely tipsy and on my way to drunk. I fingered the cream silk of my wedding dress. Or maybe I needed to consider it my not-wedding dress. I'd been all dressed and ready to go when I'd failed in my battle against the knot of tension balled like a vise around my heart. I swallowed against the rush of emotion that rose inside as my eyes traveled down the fitted bodice of my dress and bounced to the muddy splotches all over its swirling skirt. Oh yeah. I hadn't simply ditched my groom-to-be just before we got to the altar, I'd bolted in the rain. Another swallow of beer, followed with a slow sigh. What stung the most—all I felt was relief. Not regret, not second thoughts. Just pure relief.

I'd walked across the hallway at the back of the church and barged into Earl's dressing room. There he'd stood, tall and handsome with his dark blonde hair and brown eyes. It was what I never saw in his eyes when he looked at me that pushed me to tell him I couldn't marry him. When Earl looked at me, I saw a kind regard, a humored attempt to appreciate me for who I was. Yet, there was never anything close to the hot fire I'd known once upon a time with someone else. I'd apologized, but I'd also been flat pissed with him for trying to trick himself and me into thinking he really loved me.

A dash into the late afternoon rain on a cool summer day in Alaska had felt cleansing. Until I got chilled and finally ducked into this bar. I didn't even know what it was called. I suddenly recalled I didn't have a penny on me. It wasn't like I'd been carrying a purse for my aborted walk up the aisle. Oh well, oh hell. I caught sight of my reflection in the mirror behind the bar and bit back a sigh. My amber hair was a damp, tangled mess.

I didn't think much about how I looked. To be honest, it was more that I tried not to. I was as tall as most men. I ran my own construction business to boot. I tried to never let it show, but when it came to my femininity, seeds of doubt were planted firmly inside. It didn't help that all but one man treated me pretty much like a man, Earl included.

I gave my head a hard shake and glanced around the bar again, scanning the collection of people. Businessmen rubbed elbows with fishermen here. Sports reigned supreme on the televisions screens mounted at various points in the bar, and a few pool tables were clustered in the corner. That's what I'd do. I loved pool and was pretty damn good at it.

A few minutes later, I was paired up in a game with three other guys. They'd thrown a few looks askance at my wedding dress and seemed amused at playing with me. Tipsy and deep into my *don't give a damn* mode, I set out to beat them.

Roughly an hour later, I grinned as my last ball rolled neatly into a pocket corner. "Well, boys," I said, glancing among them.

The boys in question had been drinking and gotten steadily more sullen as we played. One of them, a hulking sort with dark eyes and hair, glared at me. They'd bet on this game after the first two, and I was due five dollars each from them.

Mr. Hulk, as I'd come to call him in my head, stepped close to me, too close for comfort. "No fiver from any of us. You got that?"

I was just drunk enough not to care. I stretched up to my full five foot eleven inches. He might have more bulk than me, but I was a hair taller. "Ah, I see. You only like to bet if you're gonna win? What an ass," I said, my lips curling in a sneer.

I was stretched too thin emotionally with white hot anger, a simmering anger I'd kept buried for the entirety of the two years I'd wasted on Earl, and a tad too drunk to be reasonable right now. When the jerk stepped closer and put his finger on my chest, I didn't even think. I punched him, right in the nose.

"You fuckin' bitch!" he shouted as he swiped his sleeve across his face, smearing the blood from his nose on his cheek.

He hauled off and punched me back, his fist bouncing under my eye. He had enough heft to send me tumbling to the floor, an inglorious heap of muddied silk spilling around me. I was just tipsy enough not to care that my face was throbbing. Without the mud, minus the dingy hardwood floor under me and definitely minus the crowd now gathered around, I considered the way the silk of my dress spilled in a near perfect circle would have made a great wedding photo—one of those candid shots people would love.

In a flash, Tank was there, shoving the guy who'd punched me away. Voices above me collided with each other.

"Dude, she hit me first!"

"Self defense..."

"Yeah, but she's a girl..."

"She's a fuckin' giant, and she can hit. She's no girl!"

I closed my eyes and wished I could crawl into a hole. The buzz that had kept me afloat this afternoon and evening dissolved into mortification. The jerk was right. I was a giant and no one would ever look at me and think girly thoughts.

"Amelia?"

My heartbeat came to a screeching stop and then jumpstarted with a hard kick. I'd know that voice anywhere. Through the jumble around me with Tank leaning over to ask if I was okay, that voice rang like a loud bell inside. One man. Only one man had ever looked at me with heat in his eyes, heat so hot it singed me. That man spoke my name now. I didn't have to open my eyes to know. I did anyway. Because I couldn't bear not to see him.

Cade Masters stood at the edge of the circle gathered around me, another man in a bar crowded with men. Shaggy dark brown hair, green eyes, and a body of raw muscle stood before me. My heart felt as if it had been split open. I'd loved Cade in that wild headlong way that only youth allowed. No more than seven years had passed since I'd seen him, but it felt like forever. Cade had broken my heart and walked out of my life when I was twenty-two. He hadn't just broken my heart, he'd betrayed me.

Anger flashed hot and high inside, yet I

couldn't look away. My eyes ate Cade up. He wore faded jeans, the fabric so worn it hugged his muscled legs like a caress, and a denim jacket over a black t-shirt. He had something of an outdoorsy, biker vibe. Once upon a time, he'd taken me on long rides on his motorcycle through the nearly empty highways in Alaska surrounding our home-town. He stepped through the crowd and knelt at my side, his green gaze coasting over me. "You okay?" he asked.

I nodded without really thinking about it. He lifted a hand and ran the backs of his fingers along my cheekbone. Oh right, some guy had just punched me in the face. Cade's presence had wiped my mind clean of everything else. With barely a brush of his touch, my heart fluttered and heat tightened inside.

"You sure?"

I swallowed, suddenly aware of my throbbing cheek. My entire day flashed through my mind. A gloriously shitty day. I fought against the tears, but they welled up, unbidden and beyond my control. One tear rolled down my cheek and then another and another. Of all the times and places to encounter the one and only man who still held a piece of my heart, this had to be the absolute worst.

Cade's eyes never left mine. Something flickered deep in the depths of them, but I didn't know how to interpret it. Without a word, he slipped his arm around my waist and lifted me up, bundling me into his arms as if it was the most normal thing in the world to do. "Let's get you out of here," he said and started to stride away.

Tank caught him by the arm, and Cade glanced to him. "Yeah?"

"Just making sure she's okay," Tank replied.

All I could do was nod. I was so totally *not* okay, but I was okay in the sense Tank was asking.

Tank's warm gaze held mine, this bartender who barely knew me, but had somehow known I'd had a bad day and just needed to be left in peace while I had a few beers. I should've stayed put in my seat at the bar. My raw emotions and crazy day, all of my own making if I was being honest with myself, had gotten me into this mess.

"You want the police involved?" Tank asked.

I shook my head and finally found my voice. "No. Let's call it even. I punched him, he punched me."

"You know this guy?" Tank asked next, nodding to Cade.

"Uh huh. It's okay. He's an old friend of my family's. No need to worry," I managed. On its face, my explanation was true. Cade and I had grown up together in Willow Brook, Alaska. Our families had known each other for years. Yet, my explanation left out so much of what Cade meant to me, it was almost laughable.

Tank released his grip on Cade's arm and let us be. Cade was quiet as he strode through the bar, the crowd parting around him. I could only imagine how we looked— me in my dirty not-wedding dress and him giving off his usual *back the hell off* vibes. It was a shock to see him for the first time in years and even more of a shock to be held in his arms. I felt at home in his strong embrace. He held me easily. He always had. I loved that about him. Cade was a good four inches taller than me at six foot three inches and had never cared about how tall I was. He pushed through the door of the bar, stepping out into the late evening. The rain had stopped at some point during the long hours I'd been hiding in the bar.

He paused once we were outside on the sidewalk and glanced down, his gaze catching mine. "Why are you wearing a wedding dress?"

That was Cade, never one to waste time on preliminaries. I'd loved that about him. Oh how I'd loved so many things about Cade, back before he'd left my heart bruised and battered. Right now, I couldn't seem to recall the pain. All I knew was it felt so good—so, so, so good to be with him.

Copyright © 2017 J.H. Croix

Available now & FREE!
Burn For Me

For more swoony & sassy romance, check out my website for the following stories: https://jhcroixauthor.com/books/

This Crazy Love kicks off the Swoon Series - small town southern romance with enough heat to melt you! Jackson & Shay's story is epic - swoon-worthy & intensely emotional. Jackson just happens to be Shay's brother's best friend. He's also *seriously* easy on the eyes. Shay has a past, the kind of past she would most definitely like to forget. Past or not, Jackson is about to rock her world. Don't miss their story! Free on all retailers!

For more small town romance, take a visit to Last Frontier Lodge in Diamond Creek. A sexy, alpha SEAL meets his match with a brainy heroine in Take Me Home. Marley is all brains & Gage is all brawn. Sparks fly when their worlds collide. Don't miss Gage & Marley's story!
Free on all retailers!

If sports romance lights your spark, check out The Play. Liam is a British footballer who falls for Olivia, his doctor. A twist of forbidden heats up this swoon-worthy & laugh-out-loud romance. Don't miss Liam & Olivia's story.
Free on all retailers!

Sign up for my newsletter, so you can receive information about upcoming new releases & receive a FREE copy of one of my books: http://jhcroixauthor.com/subscribe/

FIND MY BOOKS

Thank you for reading Just Us! I hope you enjoyed the story. If so, you can help other readers find my books in a variety of ways.

1) Write a review!
2) Sign up for my newsletter, so you can receive information about upcoming new releases & receive a FREE copy of one of my books: http://jhcroixauthor.com/subscribe/
3) Like and follow my Amazon Author page at https://amazon.com/author/jhcroix
4) Follow me on Bookbub at https://www.bookbub.com/authors/j-h-croix

5) Follow me on Twitter at https://twitter.com/JHCroix

6) Like my Facebook page at https://www.facebook.com/jhcroix

_____

Into The Fire Series

Burn For Me

Slow Burn

Burn So Bad

Hot Mess

Burn So Good

Sweet Fire

Play With Fire

Melt With You

Burn For You

Crash & Burn

That Snowy Night

Dare With Me Series

Crash Into You

Evers & Afters

Come To Me

Back To Us

Swoon Series

This Crazy Love

Wait For Me

Break My Fall

Truly Madly Mine

Still Go Crazy
If We Dare
Steal My Heart
Brit Boys Sports Romance
The Play
Big Win
Out Of Bounds
Play Me
Naughty Wish
Diamond Creek Alaska Novels
When Love Comes
Follow Love
Love Unbroken
Love Untamed
Tumble Into Love
Christmas Nights
Last Frontier Lodge Novels
Take Me Home
Love at Last
Just This Once
Falling Fast
Stay With Me
When We Fall
Hold Me Close
Crazy For You
Just Us

ACKNOWLEDGMENTS

Lots of readers emailed me asking if Ellie would ever get her story. If you got to this point, you know she did. ;) I knew she would, but I wasn't sure where it would happen, and then a weekend in Vegas came to life. Because everyone needs at least one weekend in Vegas!

Thank to my editor for her patience with me during editing, and to Terri D. for being an amazing proofreader.

To the detail queens: Janine, Beth P., Terri E., Heather H., & Carolyne B. Thank you!

To my family for being there in every way. That includes my dogs, one of whom is nudging me right now to finish this up and give her some love.

xoxo
J.H. Croix

ABOUT THE AUTHOR

USA Today Bestselling Author J. H. Croix lives in a small town in Maine with her husband and two spoiled dogs. Croix writes contemporary romance with sassy women and alpha men who aren't afraid to show some emotion. Her love for quirky small-towns and the characters that inhabit them shines through in her writing. Take a walk on the wild side of romance with her bestselling novels!

Places you can find me:
jhcroixauthor.com
jhcroix@jhcroix.com

f facebook.com/jhcroix

⊙ instagram.com/jhcroix

BB bookbub.com/authors/j-h-croix

Lightning Source UK Ltd.
Milton Keynes UK
UKHW011836061222
413480UK00002B/80